4/30/99

CIT
27.95

MAY 99

E

W9-BEM-254

5

BOOBYTRAP

BOOBYTRAP

A "Nameless Detective" Novel

Bill Pronzini

Thorndike Press • **Chivers Press**
Thorndike, Maine USA   Bath, England

This Large Print edition is published by Thorndike Press, USA and by Chivers Press, England.

Published in 1999 in the U.S. by arrangement with Carroll & Graf Publishing, Inc.

Published in 1999 in the U.K. by arrangement with Carroll & Graf Publishers, Inc.

U.S. Hardcover 0-7862-1718-9 (Mystery Series Edition)
U.K. Hardcover 0-7540-3703-7 (Chivers Large Print)
U.K. Softcover 0-7540-3704-5 (Camden Large Print)

The text of this Large Print edition is unabridged.
Other aspects of the book may vary from the original edition.

Set in 16 pt. Plantin by Al Chase.

Printed in the United States on permanent paper.

British Library Cataloguing in Publication Data available

Library of Congress Cataloging in Publication Data

Pronzini, Bill.
    Boobytrap : a nameless detective novel / by Bill Pronzini.
        p.   cm.
    ISBN 0-7862-1718-9 (lg. print : hc : alk. paper)
    1. Large type books. I. Title.
PS3566.R67B66   1999
813´.54—dc21   98-31480

For Sharon McCone
Who promises to keep me
in the manner to which
I'd like to become accustomed

FROM THE NOTEBOOKS OF
DONALD MICHAEL LATIMER

Tues., June 25 — 9:00 P.M.

I finished making the third bomb a few minutes ago.

Except, of course, that it isn't a bomb. It's a "destructive device." That's the official legal definition in the California Penal Code. Chapter 2.5: Destructive Devices. Section 12303.3: Explosion of Destructive Device. I know that section by heart. It was drummed into my head at the trial. I read it a hundred, two hundred, three hundred times in the prison library.

"Every person who possesses, explodes, ignites, or attempts to explode or ignite any destructive device or any explosive with intent to injure, intimidate, or terrify any person, or with intent to wrongfully injure or destroy any property, is guilty of a felony, and shall be punished by imprisonment in the state prison for a period of three, five, or seven years."

Point of law, Mr. Latimer.

Ah, but that wasn't enough for them. The destructive devices I made six years ago, the three destructive devices I've manufactured here and now, are *more* than just destructive devices. They are also Chapter 3.2: Boobytraps. Specifically, Section 12355: Boobytraps — Felony.

"Any person who assembles, maintains, places, or causes to be placed a boobytrap device as described in subdivision (c) is guilty of a felony punishable by imprisonment in the state prison for two, three, or five years." Subdivision (c) stating in part: "For purposes of this section, 'boobytrap' means any concealed or camouflaged device designed to cause great bodily injury when triggered by an action of any unsuspecting person coming across the device."

Point of law, Mr. Latimer.

Guilty as charged, Mr. Latimer.

Five years of hell in San Quentin, Mr. Latimer.

The rage is in my blood again, pounding, searing. I have the old feeling, old terror, that it will burst my head like the bulb of an overheated thermometer. I can't write any more now —

Later

Better. Calm again. Washed my face, came back and focused on the bomb, destructive device, boobytrap resting on the table. Such a simple, beautiful, deadly little object. Very soothing, especially when I imagine it in conjunction with the first device. Number one, Douglas Cotter: mission accomplished. Lying dead on his lawn with his self-righteous "You need psychiatric help, Mr. Latimer" four-eyed head blown off. Beautiful image, confirmed by this morning's newscast. But Cotter is the least hated member of the trio, a minor collaborator in their legal conspiracy. Much more satisfaction when device number three, this little sweetie right here, pretty little surprise package number three right here, makes a pincushion of Judge Norris Turnbull.

And then, ah then, the greatest satisfaction of all, when device number two, already built and installed, the biggest and best for the man I hate most, does its work. Oh, is that going to be a blast! And the best part of that one is, I'll be there when it happens, maybe even *see* it blow and his body ripped and torn and bleeding and dead. Riskiest part of the Plan, but I can't deny myself the pleasure. Thrill of a lifetime. The ultimate high — sky high. A fireworks display to dazzle the eye, soothe the soul, write finish to an enormous injustice.

I'm so eager for it that I wonder if I ought

to rethink my schedule, deliver number three to Judge Turnbull tonight. No, better not. The Plan is perfect, the timing is perfect, never tamper with perfection. Anticipation is half the fun. *Knowing* their miserable lives are in my hands, that I control their fate just as they once controlled mine. I'm the cat and Judge Turnbull is my second mouse. Toy with him one more day, let him live another twenty-four hours, and then — boom! — blow his fuzzy white head off and rip him up into little judicial pieces.

Besides, I'm tired now, and hungry. Nothing to eat since eggs and toast this morning. I need food, rest, a good night's sleep. I need to be fresh for the work and the pleasures to come.

Vengeance is mine, saith Mr. Latimer.

Boom!

Boom! Boom!

Then off to Indiana and

Boom! some more.

1

Kerry said, "I can't go."

". . . You're kidding, right?"

"I wish I was. Lord, I wish I was."

"Kerry, we've been planning this vacation for a month —"

"I'm as disappointed as you are. More."

"Good old Jim Carpenter strikes again."

"It's not his fault, this time."

"No?" I said. "Whose then?"

"Milo Fisher's."

"And who is Milo Fisher?"

"Wealthy Houston businessman. Fisher Products. That's where I have to be this weekend and next week — Houston. Texas in late June instead of balmy Baja. Lucky me."

"Lucky both of us."

"I'd get out of it if I could," she said, "but I can't. It all came up suddenly — that's the way Fisher is, Mr. Spur of the Moment. He's expanding into California, and Bates and Carpenter has a good shot at handling all of his company's West Coast advertising. With the right presentation, Jim thinks we'll land the account."

"Uh-huh."

"It's a big account. Six figures annually."

"All right," I said. "How long will you be gone?"

"I don't know yet. There'll be meetings, social functions. And Fisher is arranging a tour of their factory for us. It looks like a full business week, at least."

"Us, you said. Carpenter going, too?"

"Yes. Don't be jealous."

"I'm not jealous."

"A touch, anyway, or you wouldn't have asked if Jim's going."

"Okay, a touch. I'm always jealous when you're out of my clutches. Hot-looking number like you."

"I'll be good," she said seriously. "You know that."

"Sure I know it."

"You're not upset about this?"

"No. Business comes first for both of us — we settled that a long time ago."

"I know how much you were looking forward to our trip —"

"We'll go to Cabo San Lucas some other time. No big deal."

"You sure?"

"No big deal. When're you leaving?"

"Friday morning. There's a dinner that

night and some sort of party at Fisher's ranch on Saturday."

"Ranch, no less. One of those big Texas spreads?"

"Like South Fork, only it's near Houston."

"South Fork?"

"The Ewing ranch. You know, *Dallas.*"

"I've never been to Dallas. Who's this Ewing?"

"Never mind," she said. "Listen, I have an idea. Why don't *you* get away for a few days? While I'm gone."

"Now where would I go by myself?"

"Well . . . how about the Sierras? Fishing — you haven't been trout fishing in a long time. And you wouldn't have to go alone. Get Joe DeFalco to go with you. He's a fisherman, isn't he?"

"A lousy one."

"So you can show him up. You've already made arrangements with Tamara to cover the agency next week and your calendar's more or less clear anyway. Why not? Nice in the mountains this time of year."

"I don't know. . . ."

"No appeal at all? A few days of fishing in the Sierras?"

"A little, maybe."

"More than a little. I can see it in your

13

eyes. You *need* a vacation, you know you do, even if it's only a short one. Why don't you call Joe? See what he says?"

"All right," I said. "All right, I'll call Joe and see what he says."

DeFalco said, "I can't do it."

"Yeah, I figured as much. Short notice."

"It's not that. Christ knows I can use a few days off from the rat race and normally I could swing it, but I'm jammed on this series we're running on city politics — dissension in the mayor's and D.A.'s offices, squabbles among the Board of Supervisors, all that."

"Uh-huh."

"Don't sound so skeptical. All kinds of crap going on in this city, which you'd know about if you read the papers once in a while."

"My head's stuffed with enough crap as it is," I said. "Besides, I read one of your so-called exposés ten years ago and that's enough yellow journalism to last me a lifetime."

"Ha ha," he said. Then he said, "No kidding, I really would like to go along, but the way things are . . . Hey, wait a minute. I just remembered something."

"Good for you."

"You know Pat Dixon? One of the assistant D.A.s?"

"Talked to him a few times. Real fireball."

"Yeah, but a nice guy. He'd make a hell of a D.A., except he'll never go after the job as long as Al Ybarra has it. One of Ybarra's protégés and solidly in Al's corner, unlike some of his disgruntled coworkers."

"What's your point, Joe?"

"The point," DeFalco said, "is that Pat owns a cabin on Deep Mountain Lake in the Sierras. Know where that is, Deep Mountain Lake?"

"Not offhand."

"Near Quincy and Buck's Lake."

"Pretty country."

"That it is. Pat and his family go up there every summer, stay three or four weeks. They were supposed to leave this Saturday, but he's had to delay a few days on account of a subpoena to testify in a felony trial. He was bitching about it to me just yesterday."

"So?"

"So he's got this friend, lawyer in Sacramento, owns the cabin next to his. And the friend won't be using it at all this summer because he's involved in a complicated tax evasion case."

"Uh-huh."

15

"Cabin's just sitting there empty. Maybe the lawyer'd be willing to rent it out to the right party. Or even to a seedy private eye like you."

"For a price this seedy private eye can't afford, no doubt."

"Not necessarily. How about if I call Pat, see if maybe something can be worked out?"

"Hell, Joe, I don't know. If I can't find somebody else, I'd have to go all that way alone. . . ."

"You couldn't stand your own company for a few days?"

"Longer than I could stand yours, probably."

"Streams loaded with trout up there," he said.

"Yeah."

"Big fat rainbows and cutthroats."

"Yeah."

"Pan-fried in butter on a crisp mountain morning —"

"Okay, okay. Shut up and call Pat Dixon."

Pat Dixon said, "I think I can set it up for you."

"If it's not too much trouble, Pat."

"No trouble at all. In fact, I'm pretty sure Tom Zaleski will be pleased at the prospect."

"How much you figure he'll ask for a week's rental?"

"Don't worry about that. When were you thinking of leaving?"

"Well, any time after Friday noon."

"Saturday morning? Early?"

"Sure. Why?"

"You could do me a big favor, in that case. And in exchange I think I can make arrangements with Tom to let you stay at his place for a week free of charge."

". . . You said free of charge?"

"Except for utilities and your food and incidentals."

"Heck of a deal. What's the favor?"

"Take a couple of passengers along with you."

"Passengers?"

"My wife and son," Dixon said. "My vacation was supposed to start on Saturday, but I've got a court appearance next Monday that's likely to carry over one or two more days."

"DeFalco mentioned that."

"So Tuesday's the earliest I'll be able to get away. And my son Chuck is especially eager to get to our cabin. If you'd take Marian and the boy with you, it'll give them an extra four or five days at the lake."

"Your wife doesn't drive?"

"Not long distances or in the mountains, if she can help it. Makes her nervous. Would you mind?"

"Not a bit. Even without the free rental."

"Sure?"

"Long drives are monotonous. I'll be glad for the company."

"You'll like Marian. Smarter than I am, teaches at Dunhill Academy, and a hell of a lot better looking. She won't talk your ear off, either. And Chuck — he's twelve, well behaved, a good kid —"

"I'm already sold, Pat."

"Sorry. I get carried away on the subject of my family."

"Don't apologize. I think my wife is pretty special, too."

"Makes us both lucky men. All right, good. Let me talk to Tom, see what he says. Might take me a while to reach him if he's in court today. You be in your office until close of business?"

"I should be. If not, just leave a message with my assistant, Tamara Corbin."

Tamara said, "You better do it."

"Think so, do you?"

"Free rent on a mountain cabin, no business hassles, nothing to do all day except murder a bunch of innocent fish. . . . Hey, I

18

wish somebody'd offer me a deal like that."

"It's a deal, no question. But I'd still rather be going to Baja with Kerry."

"Sure, I hear you. But you can do it another time, right? Drive down to Baja."

"Fly down. Cabo San Lucas, all the way at the tip."

"Tourist trap, so I hear."

"Would you care if you were going there with Horace?"

"Horace could take me to Milpitas and I be smiling the whole way."

"My point exactly," I said. "It's not the surroundings, it's the company."

"So you be leaving first thing Saturday."

"Let's not get ahead of ourselves. Pat Dixon hasn't called back yet."

"He will. He better."

"Sounds like you're trying to get rid of me."

"Bet I am. Man ever needed a vacation, I'm looking at him."

"No argument. I saw the same guy in the mirror this morning."

"And don't you go sweating about things here. I'll take care of business."

"Just don't take on any million-dollar industrial espionage jobs without consulting with me first."

"Hah. Job like that ever walked in here,

we'd both pee in our pants and slip and slide on the wet spots."

"Do me a favor, Ms. Corbin. Try to restrain yourself from using such colorful language to clients while I'm away."

"Be butter, not crap, comin' out my mouth."

"I'm so relieved. Can you work Friday morning? I'd like to drive Kerry to the airport."

"No problem. Friday afternoon, too, you want to take the whole day off."

"Can you afford to miss all your Friday classes?"

"Hey, I could blow off a month's worth and still finish the semester with a top-five-percent GPA."

"GPA. Grade Point Average?"

"Right. No more A, B, C, D, and F like when you went to school."

"Back around the dawn of time."

"You didn't go to college, right? How come?"

"Not enough funds. Not enough smarts, either."

"Bull," Tamara said. "Big old brain of yours got more stuffed into it than my Pop's basement."

"If that's a compliment —"

"There goes the phone. Mr. Dixon calling

you up to say it's all arranged, what do you bet?"

I said, "So it's all arranged. I'm leaving Saturday morning."

"Perfect," Kerry said. "This is going to work out for the best after all."

"Except for one thing. For the next week or so I'll be alone in a cabin in the Sierras and you'll be two thousand miles away in Houston."

"Pining away for you the entire time."

"Likewise."

"We could always have phone sex."

"At my age? The excitement would probably bring on a massive coronary."

"Well, you call me when you get settled up there."

"I will, soon as I can."

"I'll worry if you don't," she said. Then she said, "You know, I think I envy you."

"Why?"

"A week of sitting in a boat, wandering the woods, soaking up all that peace and quiet."

"Sounds good, all right."

"Good? Compared to marinating in hundred-degree Texas heat, it sounds like heaven."

"I'd still rather be in Cabo with you."

21

"No, I think this is the better vacation for you right now. Exactly what you need. The past several months have been . . . well, pretty stressful."

"Worst damn year of my life, so far."

"That's why the wilderness is the best place for you. Up there you'll *have* to take it easy. Relax, regenerate, and have a great time doing it."

Wed., June 26 — 10:30 P.M.

I'm ready to leave. Or I will be after a few hours' sleep. Another long day, this one. But good, productive.

Third bomb, destructive device, booby-trap packed and ready. Check. Tools neatly put away in the Hefty Mate toolbox open on the floor beside me. Check. Soldering gun and spool of wire solder. Check. Aluminum canister. Check. Microswitch. Check. Six-volt battery. Check. Fresh tin of smokeless black powder, the last of the four I bought at the gun shop in Half Moon Bay. Said I was a duck hunter and loaded my own shotgun shells, clerk said happy hunting — hah! Shame, though, that I couldn't have used C-4 plastic explosive instead. More pucker power and a hotter blast — BOOM! Send them all to hell in even littler pieces. But you need connections to get C-4 and all my military ties are long severed, long dead and buried. Like Cotter and Turnbull and the others will be pretty soon.

Check.

Cardboard box filled with the rest of the

stuff I'll need. Check. Car filled with gas so I won't have to stop anywhere after I drop off the judge's surprise package. Check. Alarm clock set for three A.M. Check. Suitcase packed except for my toilet kit and this notebook. The sixth one already, six in six months. I never realized I had such an aptitude for writing, for organizing my thoughts on paper. Sometimes I think I would have benefited from keeping notebooks all along, but mostly I'm glad I didn't. I really had no use for them before they put me in prison, back when I had a life, and I want no record of the first four and a half years in that hellhole, I don't even want to think about them. The only part of my existence that matters after Kathryn and those bastard legal eagles locked me up and threw me away, the only record I'll ever need to keep, is the part since I devised the Plan.

Check.

Anything else? Nothing else.

All systems go.

I won't be sorry to leave this place, despite its positive aspects. "Charming one-bedroom seaside cottage, completely furnished," the ad in the paper read. Drafty Half Moon Bay shack with bargain-basement furnishings, no central heating, and a stove that doesn't work right. Six hundred dollars rent, in advance, even though I told the agent I'd be here less than a month. Criminal. Even so, it's better than the studio apartment in Daly City. And palatial compared to the cell in San Quentin. Away from that steel-and-concrete trap six weeks now and still the nightmares keep coming — the worst one again last night, the one where I'm still locked in that cell, crouching in a corner, the giant rats in guards' and cons' uniforms slavering, groping, biting.

This house has got plenty of privacy, at least. Nearest neighbor is a hundred yards away, and just as important, the sound of the surf is with me every minute I'm here. Freedom. All that bright blue freedom out there. And more waiting for me tomorrow, different kind but just as soothing — green and brown and blue mountain freedom, just long enough for destructive device number two to do its work. And then it's off on the open road. Like one of those old Bob Hope–Bing Crosby movies. The Road to Indiana.

Lawler Bluffs, Indiana.

Kathryn.

Does she feel warm and secure tonight, snuggled up to that bastard pharmacist of hers? Does she think I don't know she married Lover Boy after divorcing me and moved to his old hometown and had the brat she always wanted? Or is she afraid, huddled sleepless and shaking in the dark, knowing I'll come for her sooner or later? I hope she's afraid. Knows I'm out on parole, knows I'll come, is waiting with some of the same asshole-puckered terror I felt behind prison bars for those five long long long long long years.

Big part of it is *her* fault, when you get right down to it. If it hadn't been for her, the nightmare would never have happened. Bitch ruined everything, the good life we had together. Blew it all up as surely as if she'd set off a destructive device of her own. "Intent to wrongfully injure." *She's* the one who's guilty of that, not Donald M. Latimer. She's the one who should have suffered.

J'accuse, Mrs. Bitch.

Guilty as charged, Mrs. Bitch.

The sentence is death, Mrs. Bitch.

The fourth boobytrap, the one I'll assemble after I'm settled at Deep Mountain Lake, the biggest and best and sweetest of them all, is for you, Kathryn — you and Lover Boy and the brat, too, back there in good old Lawler Bluffs, Indiana.

2

Patrick Dixon was half an hour late for our Thursday afternoon meeting in The Jury Room. Which is not a courthouse chamber but a bar and grill on Van Ness Avenue near City Hall — one of several hangouts for members of the San Francisco legal profession. The place had been crowded when I arrived at a quarter to four; by the time Dixon walked in at four-thirty, there wasn't a barstool, table, or booth to be had.

Usually the atmosphere in places like The Jury Room is one of none-too-restrained conviviality. Lawyers may be serious, even solemn, in their offices and in court, but plunk them down among their own kind in a social gathering spot that dispenses alcohol and they shed their dignity as fast as any other group of imbibers. But that was not the case this afternoon. A pall of gravity and unease seemed to hang in the bar, as tangible as black crepe at an old-fashioned funeral. Talk was muted and no one laughed or even smiled much. It was like a gathering of mourners at a wake, and in a way that was just what it was. One of their fraternity had

27

died this morning, violently and horribly. Judge Norris Turnbull, a well-respected jurist who had been on the bench for more than thirty years. Blown up by a bomb in the garage of his home in Sea Cliff.

Turnbull's murder was bad enough, but what really had the lawyers spooked was the fact that he was not the first in their profession to be a bombing victim this week. Three days ago, a criminal attorney named Douglas Cotter had been ripped apart by an explosive device packed into a sprinkler on his front lawn. Two incidents so close together couldn't be coincidence, they were all saying. It had to be the work of the same individual, and that indicated a serial bomber — a madman with some sort of grudge against the legal system. Bad enough if he was after individuals related to a specific case, but what if it was random? What if the bomber hated all attorneys, all judges? Then anybody could be next. Any one of *them* could be next.

I listened to their quiet voices, felt the thin undercurrent of fear, and by the time Dixon showed I was feeling a little uneasy myself. The threat of random, mindless violence does that to you if you've been exposed to it often enough. Does it to me, anyway. No threat to me personally in this case, but

28

there had been other cases, other threats that had been intensely personal. Nothing messes with your head more effectively than the fear, however slight, that you might be the target of an unseen and unknown enemy.

In my past dealings with Dixon he'd always been animated, full of energy — borderline Type A. Today he was as subdued as the rest of the bar's patrons, tired-looking and rumpled: tie yanked loose and askew, one of his shirt buttons undone. He said, "Sorry I'm late," and lowered his raw-boned body into the chair across from me. "Christ, I need a drink."

"Name it. I'll buy."

"Irish whiskey. Bushmill's, straight up."

"Double?"

"Yeah. Make it a double."

I went and got it for him and another beer for myself. When I came back he was talking to a white-haired party at the next table, saying, "No, there's nothing yet. No specific connection between the two."

"Has to be a connection, don't you think?"

"Not necessarily. None of us knows what to think right now."

I gave him his drink and he tossed off half of it, pulled a face, set the glass down, and mauled his head with a big-knuckled hand. Nervous habit. His brown hair was short and coarse, and the mauling didn't disturb it much. If I'd had the same habit, as straight and fine as my scalp covering is, I'd have looked like an Italian version of Don King by this time of day.

He said, "Some goddamn world we live in."

"The best of all possibles."

"Norris Turnbull was a friend of mine, one of the most decent . . . ah, *damn* whoever did that to him. Damn the bugger's rotten soul."

He didn't expect an answer and I didn't give him one.

Pretty soon he said, "Sharpened steel rods, for God's sake. Can you believe that? Razor-sharp steel rods."

"Part of the bomb, you mean?"

"Loaded into a small cardboard box and left on the front seat of the judge's car. Inside his garage; bomber gained access through a side window. When Norris opened the box to look inside, it blew fifty or sixty of those rods straight up into his face."

"Jesus."

"Bastard must've really hated him," Dixon said.

Or judges and lawyers in general, I thought, but I didn't say it. "Same kind of device that killed Douglas Cotter?" I asked.

"Bomb techs aren't sure yet. Both were set as boobytraps, but the one that killed poor Doug was simpler — black powder and metal fragments packed into a lawn sprinkler and initiated by a trip wire hidden in the grass."

"Any idea who or why?"

"None yet. No warnings, no notes or calls claiming responsibility." He shook his head, took another hit of Bushmill's. "Silent type of psycho's the worst kind — I guess you know that. Intelligent, cunning, vicious, and hyped up with some kind of agenda we can't even begin to guess at yet. Unless he starts sending letters like the Unabomber, it could take weeks to get a line on him. And if he's got a string of others on his list . . ."

"What about a signature on the two bombs?"

"Too early to tell yet. That's the hope, that he's got a track record and a definite signature."

"Signature" in the case of serial bombers means the way the individual puts his device together — the kinds of connections he makes, the types of powder, cord, solder, and circuitry he uses. Each bomber's signature is unique in some identifiable way, and it seldom varies. Once the lab techs finished going over the post-blast evidence from this morning, a process that could take days, they'd feed all the pertinent details into a computer and hope for a high-probability match. Identify the bomber, and tracing and then neutralizing him would be a much easier task.

I asked, "Who's in charge of the investigation?"

"Dave Maccerone. You know him?"

"Slightly. A good man."

"The best. Charley Seltzer, the bomb squad commander, and Ed Bozeman from our office are working with him."

I knew Bozeman, too; he was the D.A.'s top investigator. "That cuts your staff pretty thin, doesn't it? Enough to affect your vacation plans?"

"Not as things stand now. I talked to the boss about it. My caseload's caught up, or it will be after the court date next week, and none of the other ADAs is on leave or due out. Ybarra says I've earned at least a couple of weeks of R&R and I'd better go ahead and take them. I didn't argue with him."

"So you're still planning to leave for Deep Mountain Lake next Tuesday or Wednesday?"

"Unless something else happens in the meantime, God forbid. Tell you the truth, I'm twice as glad now that Marian and Chuck will be riding with you on Saturday. I'll feel better with them out of the city."

"I can understand that."

"So it's all set," Dixon said. He seemed to be relaxing a little, a combination of the Bushmill's and his vacation plans. Men and women who work in jobs like his, even more than those in my profession, had to learn to compartmentalize their lives, separate the personal and the professional; if they didn't, the daily grind plus pressure situations like the one with these bombings eventually pushed them over the edge into alcoholism, breakdowns, and other stress-induced ills. "You'll pick them up at my house at nine. I can't tell you how much they're both looking forward to it, and how grateful I am."

"Glad to do it, Pat. Besides, I'm the one who should be grateful."

He waved that away. "One thing: Tom Zaleski asked me to tell you to give his property a good check-over as soon as you get there, let him know if there are any problems."

"You mean vandalism, that kind of thing?"

"Not much of that at Deep Mountain Lake, particularly with Nils Ostergaard on watch. You'll meet Nils — retired Plumas County sheriff's deputy, lives up at the lake with his wife half the year, spends the long winter months in Quincy. He keeps a sharp eye on things. No, mainly what Tom means is problems with fallen trees, the plumbing or electricity — like that."

"Sure, I'll take care of it."

"Here're his phone numbers, home and office." Dixon handed me a piece of paper along with a set of keys on a chain. "And the keys to his cabin. We traded spares years ago."

"Is there a phone at his place?"

"Yes. He'll have it activated for you."

"Should I look up Nils Ostergaard?"

"You won't need to. He'll know as soon as you and Marian and Chuck arrive, and he'll be around before you're even settled in. You'll like him. Nosy as hell, crusty, but he's got a big heart."

"Fisherman?"

"One of the most avid you'll come across. You, too, I take it?"

"But not so avid as I used to be."

"Lake, river, streams?"

"River or streams. I'm not much of a lake man."

"Me, either. Just don't ask Nils about the best spots. He knows 'em all and guards the choice ones as jealously as he would a gold hoard."

"That go for you, too?"

He showed me a lopsided grin. "More or less. Talk to Mack Judson, owns Judson's Resort. Which isn't much of one — resort, I mean. Convenience store, cafe-and-bar, eight cabins. Caters to fishermen, hikers, summer residents."

"Uh-huh."

"Tell him I said to steer you right. He'll put you in a spot where you'll catch your limit."

"All I can ask."

"So I guess that's about it," Dixon said. "Next time we get together, it'll be up at the lake. We'll have dinner, maybe do some fishing if you're still shy a rainbow or two."

"Sounds good."

He was quiet for a time, staring into his empty glass. The death of Judge Norris Turnbull preying on his mind again, I thought. "Hell," he said finally, "let's have another round before we leave. I'll buy this one."

I said, "Sure," because he seemed to need the companionship. But I didn't let him pay; buying a second double Bushmill's was the least I could do for him.

My fishing gear was stored on the rear porch of my flat on Pacific Heights. I drove over there from Civic Center and spent some time going through it, deciding what and how much I was going to take along. I hadn't had my stuff out in a while; poking through the fly case, hefting the rods, checking the reels was like renewing acquaintances with old friends. Some of the equipment was almost as old as I am, and a hell of a lot more durable.

I settled on a couple of lightweight rods, one a fly rod and the other a spinning rod with a Daiwa reel, and an assortment of wet and dry flies, most of the lures being coachmans and hoppers and rooster tails. All of the gear was my own. I did not even consider mixing in any of the items I'd liberated from Eberhardt's garage two months ago, even though his Dennis Bailey parabolic rod was better than either of mine and he'd had some fancy, beautifully tied flies that at one time I'd coveted.

Odd thing: I hadn't been able to leave his equipment for strangers to pick over, yet I couldn't bring myself to use any of it — on this trip and probably not ever. It was the only piece of him that I'd kept from his leavings. Both a memento and a memento mori — reminders of the life and the death of the man who had once been my closest friend and partner, who'd been a stranger I hadn't really known at all. His suicide was two months behind me now; there had been closure and enough time for the emotional seal to set and harden. But the reasons he had died and the way he had died would always be with me, lodged like shrapnel and providing twinges now and then. In a way it was good, necessary that I would never forget: all that he was and all that he wasn't were a lesson to me. That was why I'd kept his fishing gear, the one tangible piece of him. It was why I'd never get rid of it. And it was why I'd never use even a single item.

In the bedroom I packed the rest of what I'd need: a couple of wool shirts, two pairs of cord pants, a pair of high-topped work shoes with thick composition soles — the rocks in mountain streams are slippery and treacherous even in the summer months — and a pair of waders just in case. A light jacket and two changes of casual clothes, underwear, socks, loafers, and I was done. The thought that I wouldn't have to wear a suit or a starched shirt or a necktie for the next week or so actually made me smile.

Simple pleasures. Those and a sense of

humor are about all the armor any of us has against the demons of daylight and darkness.

I drove Kerry to SFO on Friday morning, in plenty of time to catch her noon flight to Houston. It wasn't necessary, she said, the agency would've paid for a taxi, but I insisted. I also insisted on parking the car and coming inside the United terminal with her and hanging around while she checked her bags.

"Can't bear to let me out of your sight, huh?" she said. "Are you really going to miss me that much?"

"More."

"Absence makes the heart grow fonder, you know."

"Platitudes," I said. "Who needs 'em?"

"We'll only be apart eight or nine days."

"And eight or nine long, lonely nights."

She gave a mock sigh. "Almost sixty years old and horny as a teenager."

"You wouldn't have it any other way." I pulled her close and kissed her, not chastely.

"Whew!" she said. "No more of that or we'll be arrested for public indecency."

"Call me after you get to your hotel, right?"

"First thing." She studied my face before she said, "You will have a good time in the Sierras, won't you?"

"Sure."

"I mean, it really doesn't bother you, having to go off alone?"

"I won't exactly be alone. Besides, if it doesn't work out I can always leave early. Pick up Shameless at the cat boarder's and the two of us'll pine away for you at home."

"I'm serious."

"I'll be fine," I said. "I'm looking forward to it."

"I worry about you," she said.

"Well, don't. I'm a big boy. And a quiet fishing trip is just what I need — you said so yourself."

"If you approach it in the right frame of mind."

"My frame of mind is just fine. I'll be so relaxed when I get back you'll think I've been replaced by a pod creature. Until we get into the sack, that is."

She didn't smile; she wasn't feeling humorous. "I love you," she said.

"I love you, too. Go on, get on your plane before I jump your bones again."

She kissed me as hard as I'd kissed her and hurried away to gate security. A little worried about me, all right. But she didn't need to be. I hadn't been kidding when I'd said I was looking forward to the trip. I would miss her like crazy, but even so — and this was something I'd never admit to her — I expected to have a better time at Deep Mountain Lake than I would've had struggling among the camera-slung tourists at Cabo San Lucas.

Fri., June 28 — 7:00 P.M.

The news bulletin came over the car radio as I was heading up into the mountains east of Truckee. Explosion in the garage of Judge Norris Turnbull's Sea Cliff home at seven-forty this A.M. Turnbull dead on arrival at Mt. Zion Hospital. San Francisco police refuse to speculate on a possible motive or link between this bombing incident and the one two days ago that ended the short, miserable life of Douglas Cotter. But the news reporter had no such qualms. *He* hinted at a link. Could it be the work of a mad bomber with a grudge against the law?

I laughed when I heard that. Mad bomber? Hell, no. Righteous avenger was more like it. A man with one hell of a grudge against the law, specifically Chapters 2.5 and 3.2, Sections 12303.3 and 12355 of the Penal Code and the sons of bitches who interpreted, distorted, used them like weapons to all but destroy Donald Michael Latimer.

I laughed even harder when I pictured old Turnbull lying broken and bloody with his wrinkled monkey face full of metal barbs. Always hunching forward at the trial, not like an ape but like an overgrown vulture in his black robes. Always peering down through his glasses, stern-faced, eyes like hot stones, as if he thought he was God in the judgment seat. Hunched and peered once too often, didn't you, Judge? Passed sentence once too often, didn't you, you sanctimonious piece of shit?

I sentence you to five years in the state prison on each count, Mr. Latimer.

I sentence *you* straight to hell, Judge Turnbull.

Tears rolled down my cheeks, I laughed so hard.

Two down.

Next up: Patrick Dixon.

3

Pat Dixon's pride in his family seemed to be well founded. Marian Dixon was on the easy side of thirty-five, an attractive ash blonde with intense blue eyes and an air of both friendliness and self-containment. Like Kerry, a woman with plenty of inner resources. She seemed grateful that I'd consented to shepherd her and her son to Deep Mountain Lake, but she made it plain that she wasn't convinced it was such a good idea.

"Pat says you're a godsend," she said as we loaded suitcases and boxes of supplies into my car. "He's glad to have Chuck and me leave the city right now. I wish I could say the same."

"Pretty capable guy under pressure, isn't he?"

"Yes, but it isn't his workload that worries me."

"The two bombings?"

"That's right."

"Well, there're several thousand legal professionals in the Bay Area, Mrs. Dixon. No reason to believe Pat's in any danger, is there?"

"No, of course not. It's just . . . oh, hell, I'm probably overreacting to the situation. I'll feel better when he joins us at the lake."

"Reasonable chance the bomber will be identified and caught by then."

"You think so? I hope you're right." She worked up a smile for me. "And call me Marian, will you? I'm Mrs. Dixon to my students — the more polite ones, anyway."

Chuck came out of the house, a two-story California Spanish on the back side of Mt. Davidson, lugging an armload of fishing equipment. He was as slender as his mother, animated, loaded with energy; wearing a Giants uniform shirt and matching cap that he kept taking off and then putting back on, as if he couldn't decide whether or not he wanted his head covered. He had one of those sculpted buzz cuts kids favor nowadays and he'd gotten a lot of sun recently: his scalp was a bright pink under the pale blond bristle.

Marian asked him, "Do you really need all that stuff?"

"Sure. I like to be prepared."

"Poles and tackle at the cabin, remember."

"Dad's stuff. I'd rather use mine."

"He's a fishing junkie," she said to me. "You should see his room — angling books

44

and paraphernalia everywhere."

"Hemingway in training, huh?"

"Who's Hemingway?" Chuck said, but his grin told me he was kidding.

"He's already making plans for a trip to the Florida Straits when he turns eighteen. Marlin fishing."

"Sailfish and tarpon, too. You ever go after the big game fish?" he asked me.

"Nope, I never have. Must be a thrill."

"Yeah. The biggest." He loaded his gear into the trunk. "Hey," he said, "you've got some neat stuff yourself. What kind of reel is that? Daiwa?"

"Right."

"Cool." He ran his fingers over my fly case. "You bring any PMDs along?"

PMDs were Pale Morning Duns, a type of fly. "No."

"I've got one," he said proudly. "A number eighteen Mathews Sparkle Dun with a Zelon chuck. My dad gave it to me last Christmas."

"Nice," I said.

"Yeah. I'll show it to you when we get to the lake. Say, maybe we can go out together some morning, before Dad comes up. I know a couple of good spots."

"Streams?"

"Sure. Lake fishing's okay, but streams

are where you get the big rainbows and cut-throats."

"A man after my own heart. You pick the morning, sport."

"Cool."

I glanced at Marian as we all got into the car; her expression said she thought her son was pretty special. I agreed with her. In a day and age when a high percentage of urban twelve-year-olds take and sell drugs, pack heat to school, swagger and backsass and run wild, it was a pleasure to be dealing with one who was still a politely exuberant adolescent. Kids grow up too damn fast these days, in and out of the cities; they seem to race through childhood, truncate it, so that too many of its casual pleasures are lost to them. Chuck seemed to be growing up the better way, slowly, in a nurturing environment. Pat Dixon was a lucky man, all right, but it was the kind of luck that is mostly self-made, a product of strong genes and wise choices. The Dixons, from my limited experience with them, could have served as a family values poster unit.

We left the city via the Bay Bridge and followed Highway 80 east through Sacramento and up into the Sierras. Traffic was heavy most of the way, heavy enough for a slowdown climbing to Emigrant Gap —

summer vacationers like us, cross-country travelers, gamblers on their way to the pleasure palaces of Reno. For a while Chuck kept up a running chatter that helped pass the time. He asked the inevitable questions about my profession — "What's it like being a private eye? Do you carry a gun? Have you ever shot anybody?" — and segued from there into a solicitation of my opinion on the Unabomber and what kind of individuals made bombs to blow up other individuals. After his mother put a stop to that he rattled on about fishing, about baseball. He was a Giants fan, naturally ("I hate the Braves, they're the Dallas Cowboys of baseball, you know?") and played shortstop on his Little League team ("I can field okay, but I can't hit a damn curveball to save my butt"). Once we got up into the mountains he ran out of steam, finally turned on his boom box and donned a headset and sat back to enjoy both the scenery and whatever music was ruining his eardrums. Marian and I didn't have much to say to each other, but there was no awkwardness in the silences. She was lost in her own thoughts and I was content to be where we were, on the way to where we were going.

We stopped for lunch in Truckee, then swung off onto two-lane Highway 89 and

climbed some more across high-mountain ·
plateaus ringed by peaks perennially
crowned with snowfields. Beautiful
country, this, sparsely populated, unsullied
by the grimy handprints of man. Hard
country, too, especially in winter, but there
was no deceit or treachery in it, as there was
in the cities; what you saw was what you had
to deal with, no more and no less. With each
passing mile I could feel myself unwinding a
little more, losing fragments of the hard
core of stress like shavings off a block of ice.
A week or better up here, I told myself, and
the block would have been shaved away to
nothing.

It was not yet two o'clock when we rolled
into Quincy, the Plumas county seat. Old-
fashioned little town surrounded by high-
mountain meadows and pine forests, by
cathedral peaks and the long slopes and
sharply cut valleys that formed the region's
watersheds. Big sky up here, like in
Montana — a vast, deep blue broken only
by clusters of cumulus cloud above the
windward ridges. The town itself might
have been worth a closer look, except that I
was too busy to make the effort; its one-way
main arteries were clogged with pickups,
campers, cumbersome RVs. Jammed traffic
and honking horns and gasoline fumes:

little reminders of home and the problematical legacy of Henry Ford.

We stopped at a supermarket so Marian could buy a few things and I could stock up for myself. Then we drove on to the west end of town and picked up much less crowded Bucks Lake Road. Another ten miles or so on that two-laner, and we came to a side road that branched off to the north. A sign at the intersection read: *Deep Mountain Lake — 6 Miles.*

The first four of the six were a steady, winding climb on a rough-paved surface; the last two, the road still twisty but the terrain more or less leveling off, were on hard-packed gravel that showed signs of winter-snow erosion. You would not get many motor homes or campers coming in here, I thought, and said as much to Marian. She confirmed it. There were no camping or RV facilities at Deep Mountain Lake; during the six or seven months of the year that it wasn't snow-locked and deserted, it was strictly the domain of summer residents and backcountry fishermen and hikers who lodged by the day or week at Judson's Resort.

Thick lodgepole pine forest hid the lake from us until we were almost on top of it. Then, from Chuck: "There it is!" He'd shut off his boom box and rolled down the rear window; he was animated again, excited now that we were almost there. Off where he was looking I saw flashes of bright blue among the trees. As we came around a sharp bend, the pines thinned abruptly and most of the lake was visible ahead and below, cradled like an asymmetrical bowl in a green-and-brown nest.

There isn't a High Sierra lake large or small that won't dazzle the eye of even the most nature-challenged individual. But this one was something special even by Sierra standards, the way Fallen Leaf Lake near Tahoe is something special. It reminded me a little of Fallen Leaf, in fact, in its size and shape: a mile or so long, a third of a mile wide, tightly hemmed by trees along its northern and eastern shoreline. Its color was a midnight blue so rich and deep it seemed velvety black in patches of shade at the far edges. Sunlight glinted off the water, fashioning silver streaks so bright they made me squint even though I was wearing sunglasses. The entire surface was like polished crystal, marred only by a skiff anchored near the north shore and a small powerboat moving at the western end, its wake like a stroke from a glass cutter.

The road dropped down and followed the

shoreline. The first buildings appeared ahead, set on a wide peninsula: a long, low structure with a green metal roof, a good-sized A-frame that was probably the Judsons' living quarters behind that, and eight small, plain cabins strung out on either side of a boat launch and a dock with a gas pump at its outer end. A driveway led to a parking area in front; judging from the number of cars there and fronting the cabins, the resort was both full and a popular social gathering place. A sign jutting above the roof of the main building read:

JUDSON'S RESORT
Food & Spirits
Bait • Gas • Groceries

"Food's great in the cafe," Chuck said as we passed. "Super burgers."

Beyond Judson's the road began a series of sharp loops around trees and outcrops. The first summer home was situated a few hundred yards from the resort; the rest — a couple of dozen or so — extended around the curve of the western end. All were set below the road at the lake's edge, on lots that were narrow but very wide, separated from one another by vegetation and humped ground so that each had a certain amount of privacy. The architectural styles were as different as the people who'd built them: single-story log cabins, shingle-walled and redwood-shake cottages, A-frames, and a two-story job with an alpine roof which loosely resembled a Swiss chalet.

The Dixons' cabin was a little more than halfway around: old redwood boards and shakes, dark green shutters, its roof one long forty-five-degree slant; a railed deck built on pilings, with steps leading down to a stubby dock and a shedlike boathouse. A steep drive connected the road to a slender strip of ground along the cabin's near side, hard-packed and wide enough for maybe three cars to park.

As I neared the drive Marian said, "Tom Zaleski's property is next along — you can just see the roof of his cabin through the trees. We can stop there first, if you like."

"No, let's get you and Chuck settled in first." I made the turn and eased down the gravel incline. "Nice place. You and Pat build it?"

"No. His dad built it thirty years ago and Pat inherited it. Some day it'll pass on to Chuck and then to his children — I hope."

"*I'd* never sell it," he said. "No way."

He bounced out as soon as I stopped the car, began to unload his fishing gear from the trunk. Marian said, "I wish I had half his energy."

"I'd settle for a third."

"Oh, Lord, smell that air." She seemed much more relaxed now that we'd arrived. "And not a breath of wind."

"Usually windy up here?"

"This time of day, yes."

"Hot enough for a swim," Chuck said. "After all that riding in the car, I'm ready."

"Water must be pretty cold," I said.

"Man, it's like ice. But I like it cold."

"Your swim will have to wait," Marian told him. "There's plenty to do first."

It took us three trips to carry everything inside. Then we opened windows and shutters and doors to let the fresh mountain air in to do battle with the stuffy mustiness that accumulates in houses long closed up. The cabin was good-sized: kitchen, pantry, dining room, two bedrooms with a shared bathroom between them, and a huge living room whose glass outer wall overlooked the lake. Simple furnishings designed for comfort, most of which looked old enough to also have been inherited from Pat's father.

Marian put fuses in the switch box, then tested both the electricity and the plumbing; there seemed to be no problems with waterlines, septic tank, or generator. I offered to hook up the propane stove for her, but she said she'd take care of it later. She unlocked the sliding door to the deck, led me out there. From its outer end you had a clear view of the back side of Tom Zaleski's cabin, a plain green-walled structure that sported a deck, dock, and boathouse similar to the Dixons'.

"It's small," she said, "there's just Tom and his wife, but it has all the amenities. The keys to the boathouse and Tom's boat are on the ring Pat gave you, in case he forgot to tell you that."

"What kind of boat?"

"Rowboat with a small outboard."

"Zaleski doesn't mind if I use it?"

She smiled. "As long as you buy your own gas."

Lean and wiry in his trunks, Chuck came hurrying out of the cabin. "First dip of the summer coming up," he said.

"Don't stay in," his mother told him. "Cool off and get right out."

"Okay." He crossed to the steps, paused to peer lakeward before he started down. "Here comes Mr. Ostergaard, right on schedule."

A bright red skiff with a single occupant was angling away from the last dock on the western shore, heading in our direction.

The low-pitched whine of its outboard seemed overly loud in the stillness, even across a quarter-mile of water.

"Nils Ostergaard," Marian said. "Did Pat tell you about him?"

"He did."

"A character," she said fondly. "You'll like him —"

"Hey! Hey, you guys!"

The shout came from Chuck. He was at the side door to the boathouse, excitedly waving an arm.

"What's the matter?"

"Somebody's been in here. The lock's gone."

When Marian and I got down there I saw that the door had been secured by means of a padlock through a hasp-and-eyehook arrangement. The lock was missing, all right, and the door stood open a crack. Chuck had hold of the handle and was tugging on it, but the bottom edge seemed to be stuck.

"Crap," he said disgustedly. "Who do you figure it was, Mom? Homeless people?"

"Way up here? Not likely."

"I'm gonna be pissed if they stole our boat."

I took the handle, gave a hard yank. The second time I did it, the bottom popped free and the door wobbled open. Chuck leaned inside, with Marian and me crowded in behind. There were chinks between warped wallboards; in-streaming sunlight let me see an aluminum skiff turned upside down on a pair of sawhorses. Its oars were on the floor nearby. Otherwise, the shed appeared to be empty.

"Still here," Chuck said. "Man, that's a relief."

"I don't see an outboard," I said.

"We lock it up in the storage shed under the deck. Jeez, you think they got in there, too?"

"We'll go and look."

The storage shed was built into the foundation of the cabin, with a heavy redwood door secured in the same fashion as the boathouse. The padlock was missing from the hasp there as well. I let Marian open the door and pull on a hanging cord to light a low-wattage bulb.

"Hey," Chuck said, "this is weird."

Weird was the word for it. Evidently nothing was missing from the shed, either; Marian made a quick inventory to confirm it. An Evinrude outboard, additional fishing tackle, shovels, rakes, an extra oar for the skiff, miscellaneous items and cleaning supplies were all in their places on shelves and on the rough wood floor. No sign of disturbance. No evidence that anyone had even come inside after removing the padlock.

I asked Marian what kind of locks they'd been.

"Heavy duty, with thick staples," she said. "The kind they advertise on TV as withstanding a rifle bullet."

"Maybe that's it," Chuck said.

"What is?"

"What they were after. The locks. You know, a gang of padlock thieves."

His mother didn't smile and neither did I. Heavy-duty padlocks couldn't be picked by anyone other than an expert locksmith. About the only way to open one without using a key was to hacksaw through one of the staples, which even with a battery-powered tool would take some time and effort. Why go through all the trouble if you weren't planning to commit theft? There didn't seem to be any rational explanation for it.

A gang of padlock thieves. It made as much sense as anything I could come up with.

4

Nils Ostergaard was well into his seventies, judging from the wisps of snowy hair that poked out from under his shapeless fisherman's hat, the cross-hatching of lines on his face, and the skin folds that hung from a set of bulldog jowls. Big and powerful once, still strong-looking now but leaned down to sinew and bone encased in Levi's and a khaki vest that had half a dozen bulging pockets. Age seemed not to have slowed him down much, though. He slid his skiff in alongside the Dixons' dock with the ease of long practice, hopped out, and quickly wound a short bowline around a cleat.

The three of us had gone out on the dock to meet him. He hugged Marian, whispered something into her ear that made her laugh, pumped Chuck's hand, gave me a mildly suspicious look from under wild white eyebrow tufts, and demanded, "Where's Pat?" Marian told him, and he nodded and fixed his bright blue gaze on me again. "Who's this?"

I said, "Chauffeur and squatter for a week next door," and introduced myself.

58

"He's not really a chauffeur," Chuck said. "He's a private eye."

"The hell he is."

"No bull. He's a friend of Dad's and he drove us up. Mr. Zaleski's letting him stay at his cabin for a week, free."

"Free, huh?" To me, Ostergaard said, "You don't look much like a private eye."

"You don't look much like a retired sheriff's deputy."

"Show you my badge if you want to see it."

"Show you my license if you want to see it."

"You two can show each other whatever you like," Marian said, "but don't do it in front of us."

We all laughed except for Chuck. He said, "Somebody stole our padlocks, Mr. Ostergaard."

"What's that?"

"Off the boathouse and storeroom doors. Both of 'em."

The old man scowled. "Busted in? What'd they steal?"

"That's just it," Marian said. "Nothing's missing. Not a thing."

"Damage?"

"No. It wasn't vandalism, either. Just the padlocks missing."

"Hell. Doesn't make any sense."

"We were just saying the same thing."

"Callie and me been up since late March," he said. For my benefit he added, "Do that every year, soon as the road's open. Check everything out, then keep an eye on things until Judson's opens first of May. Afterward, too. Didn't notice any missing padlocks last time I was over here."

"When was that?" I asked.

"Few days ago."

"That makes it even odder," Marian said. "Why would someone take such a risk with the lake starting to crowd up for the summer, and then not even steal anything?"

"Beats me. You check the Zaleskis' property? Boathouse and storeroom padlocks over there?"

"Not yet," I said.

"How about you and me go do that right now, private eye?"

I agreed it was a good idea, and Ostergaard led the way to a barely discernible path that wound up over the hump of wooded ground separating the two properties. He set a fast pace, climbing over rocks and plowing through scrub brush and around tree trunks; I had to work to keep up with him and I was a little winded by the time we reached the Zaleski boathouse.

Which proved to both of us that he was in better condition than a city dweller fifteen years his junior, not that I would have disputed it anyway.

A padlock was in place on the boathouse door, an old and sturdy Schlage that yielded to the key on the ring Pat Dixon had given me. Ostergaard took a look inside, shook his head to tell me that nothing had been disturbed, then took me around to the far side of the cabin to where a storage shed had been grafted onto the wall. Same thing there. Padlock in place, no apparent breach of the shed.

"Well, hell," Ostergaard said as we started back. "Kids, some sort of screwy prank — that's all I can figure."

"Local kids, you mean?"

"Probably. Lake's too far off the beaten track for outsiders to come prowling around at night."

"Could've been done during the day, couldn't it?"

"Suppose so. But I'm out and around a lot and my eyesight's as good as it ever was."

Your nose, too, I'll bet. But I kept the thought to myself.

"I catch anybody messing around again," he muttered darkly, "they'll wish they'd gone someplace else. You keep that private eye of yours open, too. Let me know if you see anything that don't look kosher."

"I'm not a Pinkerton," I said. "They're the ones who never sleep."

That got a chuckle out of him. He asked, "What's your first name again?" and when I told him he said "Nils" and shook my hand for the first time. "You were a cop once, too, am I right?"

"You're right. SFPD for a dozen years before I opened my own agency."

"Thought so. Get so you can tell one of your own."

"Biggest fraternity in the country."

"And one of the most maligned. I been retired ten years now and I'm still on the job, at least as far as my head's concerned. Once a cop, always a cop."

"It's in the blood," I agreed. "Even when the blood isn't as thick as it used to be."

"Mine's still thick enough," he said. "So's yours, seems like. Be thicker still if you got more exercise, shed that half-inflated spare tire you're lugging around inside your belt."

I didn't argue with him. He was right, and there was no malice in the advice. We knew each other now; we were comfortable with each other and would be whenever we met again. That was one of the plusses in a couple of old birds of a feather coming together: The common ground was enough for both to share and it no longer mattered which one had the biggest pecker.

The one major difference between the Zaleski cabin and the Dixon cabin was a massive elk's head and horns that took up much of the wall above the native stone fireplace. I wondered if Tom Zaleski was a hunter and it was a personal trophy. Considering the fact that he was a Sacramento lawyer, I wouldn't have been surprised to find out he'd stumbled across the animal dead in his backyard and decided to take advantage of the situation. The stuffed head wore a baleful expression and the glass eyes seemed outraged, as if the elk had been mad as hell at dying before his time. I reached up and patted his flared snout and said to him, not at all facetiously, "I'd feel the same way, brother, if some son of a bitch shot me full of holes and then cut off my head and stuck it up on a wall."

The place smelled even mustier than the Dixons'. I opened windows and shutters and doors, fired up the generator and switched on an old-fashioned ceiling fan in the front room. Then I tested the plumbing — no problem there — and hooked up the propane tank. The beer I'd bought for myself in Quincy had warmed up, but I popped the top on one anyway and slugged at it as I put the groceries away, unpacked my suitcase in the knotty pine bedroom.

Small surprise when I went to hang up a few things in the closet: The door was locked. I found the key to it on the ring and the reason for the lock as soon as I opened up. Bolted to the back wall was a glass-fronted cabinet containing two rifles, a cased telescopic sight, and a Mossberg .410 pump shotgun. Zaleski was a hunter, all right. The cabinet was locked, too, and if there was a key for that on the ring I didn't check for it. Guns don't interest me much, sporting arms not at all.

One more thing to do before I could start to relax in earnest — the property check I'd promised to make for Zaleski. I finished it in less than ten minutes. No winter storm damage that I could see and no other evident problems. About the only thing that needed attention was a collected mat of pine needles around the chimney on the roof that were already beginning to dry out. The spark arrester on the chimney's top looked okay, but dry needles are highly flammable and they ought to be cleared off as a precaution. Not by me, though, with my dislike of heights and a steep-slanted roof like this one. Marian would know somebody who could do the job — Chuck, maybe. Or Nils Ostergaard would know.

It was four-thirty by the time I finished, and I thought that if I was going to have any chance of catching Kerry at her hotel — two-hour time difference, getting on toward dinnertime in Houston — I'd better call right away. The phone had been turned on as promised and provided a static-free connection to the Houston Center Marriott. That was the good news; the bad news was that Kerry wasn't in. I left a safe-arrival message and the phone number with the hotel operator.

I locked up and set off on foot for Judson's Resort. It was a fine evening for a stroll — some of the needed exercise Nils Ostergaard had alluded to. The day was still warm and the thin air was so rich in the scents of pine resin and lake water that it went to your head, gave you a kind of natural buzz.

There were two men inside the store half of the main resort building when I walked in. One, a shaggy, barrel-chested guy about my age, stood behind the counter; the other, dour and angular, wearing a fisherman's slouch hat, was bent over in front of a cooler marked *Live Bait*. Through a doorway on the right, a noisy bunch — men and women both — were grouped along the cafe's bar counter, most of them clutching long-necked bottles of Miller and Bud.

The shaggy guy said cheerfully, "Help you?" as I came up to the counter.

"You can if you're Mack Judson."

"In the flesh." He grinned and patted the paunch that hid his belt buckle. The hair on his hands and arms and curling up through the neck of his polo shirt was as thick and black and coarse as bear fur. "If you're looking for accommodations, I'm afraid you're out of luck. We're full up."

"I've got a place to stay," I said, "thanks to Tom Zaleski and Pat Dixon." I introduced myself and explained how I happened to be there.

"Any friend of Pat's," he said, and grated my finger bones in a bearlike paw. "Welcome to God's country, my friend."

"Thanks. Glad to be here."

The angular customer had sidled over next to me. He nudged my arm and asked, "What line're you in?" The question came with a distillery aroma. Sour-mash bourbon.

"Does it matter?"

"I like to know what a man does for a living."

"What do I look like I do?"

"Cop," he said immediately.

"Close enough. I'm a private investigator."

"The hell you say. What brings a private eye up here?"

"Same thing that brought you."

"The fishing, huh?"

"That's right."

"A private eye that fishes. How about that."

"Lake or stream?" Judson asked me.

"Stream. Pat Dixon says you can point me to a couple of good spots."

"That I can."

"Good spots for the likes of us," the angular guy said. He was about forty, thin-lipped, hollow-eyed. Long, flattened ears and a pointy jaw gave his head a squeezed look. "He reserves the best places for himself and his cronies, don't you, Mack?"

Judson's expression remained affable, but dislike leaked through at the edges. "Well, I'll tell you, Mr. Dyce," he said. "My wife and me been running this resort twenty-two years and nobody who took my advice ever went home without his limit."

"Limit, sure. Little brookies and rainbows. Easy catches."

"Easy? Easy's when you go to a trout

farm. Come up here, you work for every fish you take. Harder you work, the more you get for your effort — like anything else in this life."

"Meaning I oughta go hiking around the backcountry on my own. I don't know these mountains, I could get my ass lost or break a leg or something."

Judson shrugged. "Accidents can happen anywhere, if you're not careful. Point is, even if I told you where you might catch a five-pound cutthroat, you'd have to work like the devil to get there. Risk your ass, if you want to put it that way. And you might not catch that five-pounder anyway."

"Suppose I paid you to guide me?"

"I'm not a guide. I'm a resort owner."

"Close-mouthed one, you want my opinion," Dyce said. He turned his attention my way again. "So what kind of private eye are you?"

"I don't understand the question."

"What kind of jobs you specialize in? Divorce work?"

"No."

"Get the dirt on some poor bastard for his bitch of a wife?"

"I said no."

"Bodyguarding, that kind of thing?"

"Not that, either. Most of my business is

skip-tracing and insurance-related."

"Minding other people's business. Isn't that what a private eye really does?"

"Professionally, maybe. Personally I mind my own business."

"You telling me to mind mine?"

"I'm not telling you anything, Dyce."

"Wise guys," Dyce said. "Man can't get away from wise guys no matter where he goes."

I didn't say anything. Neither did Judson.

Dyce looked from one to the other of us, curled his lip the way his type does when feeling superior, and stalked out. The screen door smacked shut behind him, loud as a pistol shot.

"What's his problem?" I asked Judson.

"Pretty obvious, isn't it? Mr. Fred Dyce is an asshole."

"Other than that."

"I couldn't tell you. Chip on his shoulder a yard wide, who knows why. Maybe because he drinks too much, maybe from breathing all that smog in L.A. That's where he's from."

"Spoiling for a fight, I'd say."

"That's what I'm afraid of — that somebody'll provoke him without even meaning to. He's been here two days, already seems like two weeks. But I can't kick

69

him out for what might happen, much as I'd like to. He's the kind that'd sue."

"His first time here?"

"And his last," Judson said. "He calls up next year, we're full the entire season. Well, hell, why let one schmuck spoil it for the rest of us? Everybody else staying here gets along fine. Come on, I'll introduce you to Rita — that's my missus — and the folks in the cafe. Buy you a beer, too, if you drink beer."

"I drink it."

"Good. It's a tradition we got here: first beer's on Mack and Rita."

I didn't feel much like socializing — I was in a mood for my own company tonight, after the long drive — but Judson had been offended enough by Dyce without my adding a refusal of his hospitality. I followed him into the cafe.

Rita Judson, a sinewy brunette with a sharp eye and an unflappable manner, was behind the bar. I found out a little later that she and Mack handled all of the resort duties except for cooking, waitressing, dishwashing, and maid service; they had a hired couple who took care of those chores. Rita shook my hand with a grip as firm as any man's, welcomed me to Deep Mountain Lake, and served me an ice-cold bottle of Bud. Mack introduced me to the seven other people at the bar, four summer residents and three short-stay fishermen. They were all just names and faces at first, except for two other first-timers like Dyce and me. One was on the lean side of forty, the back-slapping salesman type, friendly but in a sly, pushy way. Cantrell, Hal Cantrell. The other was Mr. Average: medium height, medium weight, medium features, medium coloring, of an age anywhere between forty and fifty. The kind of individual who fades into the background in any social situation and disappears completely when a score of people are present. He didn't have much to say — the complete opposite of Cantrell. The only thing about him that made any impression on me were his eyes, gray eyes so pale they were almost colorless, like smoke just before it fades away. His first name was unusual enough to stick in my memory: Jacob. But I heard his last name only once and couldn't remember it afterward.

Naturally there were questions for me, a spate of them when Judson announced my profession, but then things settled down into a companionable discussion of fishing matters — the old debate over whether it's best to fish upstream or downstream, the relative merits of both dry flies and live bait

71

in the streams that fed Deep Mountain Lake, that kind of thing. Once the others realized I had enough knowledge to lift me out of the rank amateur class, I was accepted without reservation.

Judson gave me a hand-drawn map — actually a photocopy of one from a folder behind the bar — that showed side roads and trout pools in the area. I listened to advice from him and a couple of the others on which spots were best this year for cutthroat browns and rainbows. The most votes went to a pool labeled Two Creek Bar.

"It takes some hiking," Rita said, "about a mile and a half crosscountry, but the terrain's not too rough."

"I don't mind a good hike."

"Two Creek's the place to go, then."

"I'll give it a try first thing tomorrow."

I bought a round of beers and then managed to slip away more or less gracefully, in deference to my growling stomach.

Chuck came knocking at the door as I was broiling a small steak and making a salad to go with it. "Mom sent me over to invite you to dinner tomorrow night," he said when I let him in.

I gestured at my fixings. "Good thing it's not tonight."

"Yeah, that steak smells good. We're having chili. Tomorrow it'll be trout. Pan-cooked on the Weber."

"Sounds tasty."

"Tasty? Man, they'll be *outstanding.*"

"What time?"

"Seven, she said."

"I'll be there."

"Cool. She talked to Dad a little while ago."

"Everything okay back home?"

"Sure. But they haven't caught that asshole yet. You know, the bomber."

"Any new leads?"

"Not yet. Dad thinks something'll break pretty soon. You know where you're going first?"

"Going?" Kids can switch subjects fast enough to throw an Einstein off stride.

"In the morning. Where you're gonna fish."

"Oh. Place called Two Creek Bar."

"Yeah, that's an okay spot."

"But not one of the best?"

"Nah." His eyes took on an anticipatory shine. "The best, the absolute best, bar none, that's where I'm going."

"That what it's called? Bar None?"

"Huh?"

"Never mind. Dumb joke."

"It doesn't have a name," he said. "Dad found it a few years ago, caught a three-pound cutthroat right off the bat. Last year I hooked one that weighed three and a quarter. Man, I can't wait to get out there!"

"I don't suppose you'd be willing to share the secret."

"Nah, it's just for us. But there's a spot I found that's almost as good that I'll show you. You still want to go out, just the two of us?"

"Sure. Any time."

"How about Monday morning?"

"If we're not too full of tomorrow's catch."

"Can't ever get too full of pan-cooked trout."

"No argument there. Okay, Monday morning it is."

"Way cool."

After supper I sat on the deck watching night settle around the lake. It was chilly with the sun gone and the sunset colors fading, the sky darkening into a deep, velvety indigo; there was a wind off the water now, thin and gusty, with an edge I could feel through the lined jacket I'd put on. I thought that I ought to go inside, build up the fire I'd started earlier, but I wasn't ready to do that just yet. Nice out here, despite the temperature. Peaceful. The kind of night in the kind of setting that takes hold of your thoughts, turns them inward.

Indigo modulated into purple, then into star-hazed black. No moon yet, but the starshine was so bright it cast a whiteness over lake and trees and mountain peaks that made them seem almost pearlescent. The sky was so clear you could see the broad, awesome sweep of the Milky Way. When you deal with ugliness and evil as often as I had, for as many years, you can lose sight of how much beauty and serenity there is in the world. Places like this remind you of that fact — just the sort of reminder I needed at this point in my life. It helps put everything back into a proper perspective.

From somewhere — Judson's, probably — I could hear music, so faint that the melody wasn't identifiable. Otherwise, except for the soughing of the wind in the pines and the intermittent splash of a fish jumping after insects, the night hush seemed thick and palpable, a gentle pressure against the eardrums. There was a lonesome quality to both the stillness and the mountain vastness: I missed Kerry and wished she were here to share this time with me. But it was a mild sort of yearning, almost pleasurable, like the anticipation of something you want very much and know for certain you'll soon have.

Mainly I was at ease. With myself as well as my surroundings. All the sad, hurtful things that had troubled my life seemed far away and less important or not important at all; even Eberhardt's sudden suicide and the bitter reasons behind it, only two months in the past and the source of so much internal chaos at the time, had a remoteness now, here, that led me to wonder briefly if I were turning callous in my incipient old age, walling myself off from the strong feelings that had always been an integral part of my nature. The answer, I decided, was no. My feelings, like a lot of my opinions, were as strong as ever; it was the interpretation I put on them, how I let them affect me, that was undergoing a change.

Mellowing. Well, maybe, but that was only part of it. There was something else, something deeper, that I was only just beginning to understand. Give it time. It would become clear to me eventually.

My, my, I thought then. Learning patience and insight, too, after nearly sixty years? Wonders never cease.

I laughed out loud, gazing up at the Milky Way. I hadn't felt this good, this secure, in a long time.

FROM THE NOTEBOOKS OF
DONALD MICHAEL LATIMER

Sat., June 29 — 8:45 P.M.

Damn Dixon!

I had everything planned so perfectly. Timing, setting, method, everything. And he's spoiled it by staying in San Francisco and sending his wife and kid up here with a detective, of all things. A fucking private cop.

Does he suspect? Has he figured some of it out? I don't think so. He wouldn't have let his family come at all if he had an inkling that he was a target. Unless he figures I don't know about his vacation home and my plan is to boobytrap him down there, the same as Cotter and Turnbull, and it's his way of getting wife and brat out of harm's way. That would explain the private cop. But if Dixon reasoned that far, then he'd also have to have a pretty good idea Donald Michael Latimer is the man behind the bombs, excuse me, destructive devices. And a pretty good idea of the rest of it, too, the *reason* I built the devices for Cotter and Turnbull the way I did and what's in store for him. And he doesn't know who or why, or else a police bomb squad would have arrived at the lake instead of the family and my name would be all over the news.

All right. He doesn't suspect. The wife and son came up without him because he has a court date next week and he didn't want them to have to delay their vacation, and the private cop drove them up as a favor in return for the use of somebody's cabin, and Dixon will be driving up alone next Tuesday or Wednesday. The truth? It's what the cop told Mack Judson and it sounds reasonable enough.

So now what am I going to do?

I can't make up my mind. But I better make it up soon.

Option number one: Remove the device, then drive all the way back to the city and deliver it to Dixon at his house or some other place he hangs out. Risky to go after it now that it's in place, with the woman and boy at the cabin. Risky to move it even a short distance with it armed, much less transport it over three hundred miles. I can disarm it, but that's risky, too. Besides, it belongs where it is. It's *right* where it is.

Option number two: Proceed according to the Plan. Stay put, don't do anything except wait for Dixon to show up and claim his ticket to hell. Tuesday or Wednesday, four or five days. I can wait that long. I waited five goddamn years, didn't I? Of course the danger in waiting is that wifey or sonny triggers the Big Boom before daddy shows. It could happen. Not too likely, not where and how the boobytrap is set, but it could happen. And if it does, it'll be twice as difficult targeting Dixon again. Should I take the chance?

Option number three: Find a way to lure Dixon up here immediately. Fake emergency, something like that. Tricky. I can't think of anything that would bring him running without also making him suspicious when he finds out there's no emergency after all. Once he's here he has to have his mind on R&R, nothing else, otherwise the device doesn't get triggered. Bad idea. Scratch that one. When the bastard comes he has to come on his own hook. Hah!

The second option is the one that makes the most sense. Leave the package where it is, wait it out, trust that nobody but Dixon gets a faceful of hell. The longer the anticipation, the sweeter the revenge.

5

The road that led around the east end of the lake into the wilderness was narrow, heavily pitted in some places, rock-strewn in others. My old car wasn't right for it; I had to do some fancy maneuvering to keep from tearing up the undercarriage, maybe puncturing the oil pan and stranding myself out there. Three miles in, the track was so narrow and tree-hemmed that an oncoming vehicle of any kind would've created a two-car gridlock.

I bumped around a sharp left-hand turn and finally emerged into a small grassy glade. According to Judson's map, this was as far as you could drive. It surprised me a little to see a beat-up, ten-year-old Chrysler LeBaron and a Chevy four-by-four already parked there. I'd left the cabin at first light, and the sky was still pale and the shadows long and deep under the pines. So much for the idea of stealing a march on anybody else who might be headed for Two Creek Bar.

I slanted in next to the four-by-four and popped the trunk lid. Preparations first. I was wearing a thin cotton shirt under a heavy wool Pendleton that I could strip off when the day warmed, heavy cord pants with my fish knife sheathed at the belt, the high-topped work shoes, and my old slouch hat; I added a lightweight canvas creel on a strap slung over my shoulder, then buttoned a couple of nutrition bars into one shirt pocket and a flat plastic case into the other. The case held six lures — nothing fancy this first time out, just a pair of Royal Coachmans, a pair of Light Cahills — #12 and #14 — and a Gray Hackle and a Spider. When you fish mountain streams, particularly ones you've never seen in unfamiliar territory, you're well advised to keep one hand free to help you move from rock to rock, around trees and other obstacles. And the fewer items you have attached to your clothing, the better the odds against snags and torn fabric.

The bamboo rod and Daiwa reel came out next. I'd already rigged a leader and hook to the .009 monofilament line, tied off with a blood knot; I made certain the reel's bail was thumbed-down tight and then hefted the rod, made a few practice flips to test its resiliency. It felt fine in my hand. Some of the old sportsman's excitement began to work in me. I'd almost forgotten how much pleasure a man could derive from being out in the woods like this, on his way to a trout pool.

Two deer trails led off at angles from the glade, like spokes from the hub of a wheel. The one to the northwest was the way to Two Creek Bar. I set out along there, through ferny underbrush, walking carefully and watching the tip of the rod. Break your favorite rod the first day out and you might as well quit and go home because you're in for miserable luck. Fisherman's superstition, one I'd never argue with.

The trail led gradually, then more steeply, up to higher ground. The first half to two-thirds of a mile was through dense forest, mostly lodgepole and tall, straight sugar pine; after that the trees thinned and the terrain opened up into a long, sloping meadow spotted with boulders and outcrops. Yellowed grass, dusty and pungent, with a deadfall at one end. High fire danger here. But this country was loaded with deadfalls and tinder-dry grass and brush. Every summer would be just a little nerve-wracking for anyone who lived in the more remote sections of the Sierras.

I quartered downslope to the west. Birds chattered now and then; otherwise, the morning held an almost preternatural hush. The sun had bobbed up now, its light dazzling on the distant peaks, a rich mellow gold on the meadow grass and across the tops of the pines at higher elevations. The air was thin and sweet and cold. It burned in my lungs, had me panting even though I was not setting much of a pace. *Come on, fats. Nils Ostergaard's got twenty years on you and he could probably hike five times as far without breaking a sweat.* The thought kept me plodding onward instead of taking a rest stop.

The ground continued to slope downward, through more woods. I heard the stream before I saw it, the good icy rush of water tumbling over rocks. Another fifty yards and the first silvery flashes appeared among the shadows; another fifty after that and I was out onto its bank, grinning at the stream as if it were Dr. Livingstone and I was Mr. Stanley.

Twenty feet wide at this point, the stream was clear and shallow and fast-moving. And clean, literally above pollution. Still grinning, I headed upstream with the creek's voice in my ears. Trees and undergrowth clogged the bank in places, so that I had to wade through the chill water. For the most part, though, it was an easy hike, past small pools and riffles, shallows and eddies, flats and glides.

At the end of a quarter mile the creek

hooked left, and when I came around the bend I was looking at a wide, deepish pool. Above it, on higher ground where runty digger pine grew, a second creek, quick and narrow, joined this one from the east; at the juncture there was a curling gravel bar that had given the spot its name. Sunlight glinted off bits and pieces of mica rock along the bar. I wondered if maybe there were flakes of gold there, too, washed down from the higher elevations. Gold collected in such bars, sometimes in quantities large enough for backcountry prospectors to eke out a living. Not here, though, or the spot wouldn't be on Mack Judson's map. Gold hunters are considerably more jealous of their favorite haunts than fishermen are of theirs.

I waded out to a flat rock at the pool's edge, squinting against quicksilver flashes coming off the surface, and hunkered down to peer into the depths. Clear all the way to the bottom, three feet or so here and likely deeper in the middle. Trout in there, all right, even though I couldn't see them. You can feel their presence in pools like this one, shadows moving among other shadows beneath the light.

I took out the lure case. The Gray Hackle struck me as my best bet in water like this, with the air as still as it was; I tied it on and made my first cast, downstream toward where a lopsided pine jutted out from the far bank. It didn't get me anything, so I reeled in and made another cast, this time dropping the fly in the pool's center. I drew it along about a foot below the surface, slowly, letting the water give it plenty of sideways twitch and sway. Nothing. I tried again, a little farther down and to the left of the canted pine.

Small tug on the line as I reeled in, then another, harder bump. I snapped the tip of the rod upward, striking against the bite. The rod jerked and shimmied in my hand. In the next second I saw the fish just under the surface, a darkish movement coming my way, and then he was out, hanging and twisting, his square tail slapping the water so hard spray went flying halfway down the pool.

Oh, man, he was a beauty. A big cut-throat, eighteen or nineteen inches long and at least two pounds, maybe as much as three — a brilliant orange and brightly speckled, with a bullet head and a broad tail.

Gone again, then, and the rod bent and the reel made a ratchety buzzing noise before I could snub the line. He was heading for a stony riffle at the far end of the pool. I hauled on the rod, got him turned; he jumped again, arching, throwing spray. But he was hooked good. The rest of the struggle was brief, almost anticlimactic.

I brought him out and caught him with my left hand, held him around the middle. Then I worked the rod into the crook of my right arm and used the fingers of that hand to remove the hook. Some fine fish. I could work this spot and a dozen others the entire week I was here and not snag another of this size. Pure sweet luck to take such a prize in the first five minutes.

The feel of his body was hard and firm, the kind of mountain trout whose flesh flakes like a cracker when it's cooked. The best eating there is. My mouth began to water just thinking about it. And yet I couldn't seem to take the next step, which was to unsheath my knife and kill the fish by bashing its head with the weighted handle. I kept standing there, holding him, feeling him squirm, feeling the life in him, watching his mouth and gills open and close, open and close as he sucked air.

Come on, I thought, get it over with.

Yeah, I thought. Breakfast right here in your hand, meal fit for a king.

Aloud I said, "Fish, we're both lucky as hell this morning," and I leaned down and released him. Quick flash of orange and he was gone for good.

I sighed and straightened up. For about five seconds I was mildly disgusted with myself; then a kind of elation began to work in me and all of a sudden I felt fine, really happy. So happy and free and full of life, like that beauty of a trout swimming around somewhere beneath the sunbright surface, that I laughed out loud — a laugh like the bark of an old sea lion. That was me, by God, an old sea lion sunning its fat on a rock —

"Hey, you okay down there?"

The voice came from behind and above me, close enough to make me jump and then twist around. A guy carrying a fly rod in one hand and a polypropylene tackle box in the other was standing on an outcrop about twenty yards away. Had been standing there, anyway, no telling how long; now he stepped off and made his way down over a scatter of loose rock and gravel toward where I was.

I went to meet him on the bank. At first I took him for a stranger, but when we were close enough I recognized him — another of the first-timers, the pale-eyed Mr. Average. Jacob something; I still couldn't remember his last name.

He said in his medium voice, "What'd you do it for?"

"Do what? Oh, the fish."

"Looked like a nice cutthroat. You're not one of those catch-and-release types, are you?"

"No." At least, I thought, I didn't used to be.

"So how come you let it go?"

I shrugged. "Momentary whim."

"Why'd you laugh like that, afterward?"

"No particular reason. Just feeling good."

"I thought maybe you were having some kind of attack." He seemed puzzled by what I'd done, as if he couldn't conceive of anyone behaving that way. It made me a little uncomfortable. A touch embarrassed, too, in spite of myself, as if I'd been caught performing an unnatural act or exhibiting signs of an acute mental disorder.

"One of those mornings when you're glad you're alive," I said. "I figured the trout deserved to enjoy it, too."

"Why? It's nothing but a fish."

"A fish is something. One of God's creatures."

"You should've killed it," he said.

"But I didn't." Strayhorn, that was it. Jacob Strayhorn. "My business either way, right? I'm the one who caught it."

He stared at me for a few seconds, then made a movement with his head, a kind of cranial shrug, and said through a small, pale smile, "Sure, that's right. Your fish, you could do whatever you wanted with it."

To change the subject I asked, "How about you? Any luck this morning?"

"Not much. Couple of brookies."

"Well, it's early yet."

"You going to keep working this pool?"

"For a while."

"If you hook that brown again, what'll you do?"

One-track mind. "Chances are I won't."

"But if you do. Let it go again?"

"Why does it matter so much to you, Strayhorn?"

"It doesn't matter. I'm just curious."

"I don't know what I'd do. Does anybody know exactly what he'll do in every situation?"

"Some people do," Strayhorn said. "I do."

"Every situation, every time?"

"That's right."

"Circumstances, intangibles — they don't matter?"

"Not when you've got a definite purpose."

"Like fishing."

"Fishing, hunting, whatever. You ought to be that way, too, the kind of business you're in. How can you be a cop and not be sure of yourself, what you're doing every minute?"

"I didn't say I didn't know what I was doing. I said I don't always react the same way. It's a mistake to equate purpose and dedication with an inflexible mind-set. A good cop keeps an open mind."

"The way you did with that fish," Strayhorn said. "Momentary whim, no real purpose or objective."

He smiled to take the sting out of the words, but they annoyed me just the same. *He* annoyed me. In not much more than five minutes Mr. Not So Average had pried open the drain on my high good mood.

I said, "Suppose we drop the subject, okay? Get on with what brought us out here." I hefted my rod and started to turn away from him.

"Answer one question first," he said.

"All right, one question."

"You ever do anything like that with a lawbreaker?"

"Like what?"

"Let him go. Somebody you caught, somebody who committed a crime. A man instead of a fish."

It threw me for a few beats. There was no way he could know about recent events in my life, but in his irritating fashion he'd managed to cut straight to a still-tender nerve. "No," I lied. "Never."

"But you might someday. You're capable of it. If the circumstances and intangibles are right."

I didn't say anything.

"I wouldn't. No matter what." He laughed abruptly and then said, "I think I'd make a good cop myself. Maybe a better one than you."

"The take-no-prisoners kind? The kind that uses fists and nightsticks instead of reason and common sense? I don't think so, Strayhorn. Whatever you do for a living, I hope like hell it has nothing to do with law enforcement."

"It doesn't," he said, and laughed again. Then, as I swung away from him, "Nice talking to you."

"Yeah."

He let me get out onto the rock again before he offered up his parting shot. "I still think you should've killed that fish," he said.

He went off downstream without a backward glance. Leaving me to stand there with a sour taste in my mouth and nothing left of the good-to-be-alive feeling except a memory.

It was ten-thirty when I got to Judson's. I parked in the lot and walked around to the gas dock with the five-gallon can I'd found in Zaleski's boathouse and put in the car earlier. Hal Cantrell, the talkative glad-hander, was there ahead of me, pumping unleaded into the Johnson outboard on his rented skiff. He gave me a rueful smile as I came up.

"Man," he said, "you see the gas prices here?"

"Not yet. Pretty stiff?"

"Three bucks a gallon."

"Well, it's a long haul in here from Quincy."

"Still. Three bucks a gallon." He shook his head. "Any luck out at Two Creek Bar?"

"Not much," I said. I hadn't done much more fishing after the episode with Strayhorn, and what little I'd indulged in had not produced another catch. Just as well. I'd probably feel like going out again tomorrow, but for today I had lost my taste for the sport. "How about you? Find a good spot?"

"Fair. Little inlet on the east shore. Don't tell anybody, but I'm the lazy kind of fisherman. Rather find a shady spot on the lake, sit in a boat and drink beer for breakfast and contemplate my sins."

"Doesn't sound bad to me."

"It's not. I work hard enough at home — my wife sees to that. The one week a year she lets me off by myself, I take full advantage."

"Where's home?"

"Pacifica. Not far from your bailiwick."

"I know it well."

"Not a bad little town, but the fog gets to you after a while. That's why I come up to the mountains on my fishing trips. I'm in real estate, by the way. I'd give you one of my cards, but I don't suppose you're in the market for coastal property?"

"Not right now. Someday, maybe."

"Well, look me up if that day comes. San Mateo Coast Realty, Pacifica. Put you on to something nice and affordable."

"I'll remember that."

He finished with his outboard, shut off the pump, and peered at the total. "Thirteen-sixty," he said, shaking his head again. "Pay inside. Judson's on the honor system."

"Faith in his fellow man."

"Wish I had it," Cantrell said. "I'll bet he gets underpaid or stiffed altogether more than a couple of times a season. At three bucks a gallon, I'm tempted to under-report myself."

"But you won't."

"Nope. I'm not into petty crime." A grin stretched the broad oval of his face. "The big stuff, now . . ."

"Big stuff?"

"You know, major scams. That's what I'd get into. If you're going to run a risk, you might as well do it for the biggest possible return."

"And the biggest possible penalties."

"If you get caught."

"Most scam artists do."

"But not all of them," he said. "You don't think I might've already taken the plunge, do you?"

"I don't know," I said. "You tell me."

Another grin; he put his right hand over his heart and said solemnly, "In the famous words of a famous man, 'I am not a crook.' "

"A famous man who didn't get away with it."

"No? He got caught, sure, but then he was pardoned and handed plenty of money and a comfortable retirement and a library to house his papers, and when he died he was eulogized as a great statesman by a bunch of other statesmen who claimed *they* weren't crooks, either. Who says crime doesn't pay?"

Cantrell wandered off to pay his tab, and I thought as I unhooked the hose: Another strange bird. Deep Mountain Lake seemed to attract them; something in the thin air, maybe — a migratory lure similar to the smog or whatever atmospheric mixture brought wackos from all over the country flocking to L.A. I wondered how many more of the apparently well-wrapped folk I'd met last night would turn out to be flakes once I got to know them better. I wondered if Nils Ostergaard and Marian and Pat and even Chuck would turn out to be flakes. I wondered if I'd wound up at Deep Mountain Lake because *I* was a strange bird myself.

After that, I stopped wondering. There are some avenues of speculation that are better left barricaded with *Do Not Enter* signs.

Sun., June 30 — 12 noon

That private cop worries me.

I'm not sure why. He's porky, he must be close to sixty, he moves as though he'd have trouble getting out of his own way, and he's got a soft side, yet there's something about him that makes me nervous. Something in his eyes. You look into them and you can see that he's intelligent, good at what he does, but it's more than that, it's a kind of steel inside all that flab and sentimentality. Like the old cons in prison, the ones who'd seen it all and done it all that you didn't dare provoke, no matter how frail they seemed. This one, this private cop, would make a deadly enemy.

I keep thinking about yesterday afternoon, when the kid found the boathouse padlock missing and first the cop and then old man Ostergaard started nosing around. They had no idea I was watching through my binoculars, anchored over on the far shore, but I can't chance a regular surveillance or one of them is sure to become suspicious. The old codger worries me a little, too, but mainly it's the private cop.

He's the one I've really got to watch out for.

Careful. Very careful from now on. I'm just another fisherman. Keep everybody thinking that, keep the stage set just as it is, and when Dixon shows next Tuesday or Wednesday it'll be party time. A surprise blowout nobody around here will ever forget.

6

Tom Zaleski's boat, like Tom Zaleski's summer tenant, had seen better days. It was a twelve-foot aluminum skiff, dented on the starboard side and on the prow; but it didn't seem to have any holes in its bottom, and when I floated it out alongside the dock and then stepped down gingerly into the stern, it wobbled and sank a few inches but stayed afloat. The ten-horsepower Johnson affixed to it was at least twenty years old; Zaleski seemed to have taken reasonably good care of it, though, and had thought to wrap it with plastic sheeting for the winter. A pair of emergency oars tucked under the seats looked as if they had been hand-carved in the days of King Arthur and then made the principal weapons in a series of violent jousting matches. I hoped I would not have occasion to use them.

I gassed the outboard, primed it, and yanked the starter rope. An emphysemic cough was all the response I got. I sat there in the hot midday sun and primed the thing twice more and yanked on the rope maybe fifteen times before it finally came alive in a chattering rumble, only to croak again four or five seconds later. Three more pulls resurrected it, and this time it clung precariously to life, hacking and wheezing all the while. I held its tiller for a minute or so, trying to decide if I really wanted to risk taking the old fart out onto all that bright blue water and having it expire on me once and for all somewhere in the middle. Well, what the hell. A little adventure is good for the soul, right?

I pushed away from the dock, eased the throttle up to crawling speed. The Johnson kept right on muttering and stuttering. So I throttled up a little more and worked the tiller and pretty soon we were scooting right along, the engine seeming to gather strength and vigor from the exercise. At least it no longer complained as loudly as it had at the dock.

Out on the lake the air was cooler and the breeze felt good on my face. By the time I'd veered over toward the west shore I was a fine old hand at the helm, Captain Somebody-or-other. There were only two other boats out, both on the east end near Judson's; I had this section all to myself. I skimmed along a hundred yards offshore, checking out the summer homes down that way. A couple were large; one had a terracelike dock that jutted forty feet into the water. Some people were having their lunch out there; they waved and I waved back. Ahab in his longboat, saluting the crew. More waves came from an elderly couple sitting on the deck of the last cottage at that end: Nils Ostergaard and his wife, Callie. Ostergaard had a pair of binoculars looped around his neck and I'd have given odds that he'd been watching me during most if not all of my launching difficulties. He didn't miss much, especially with other forms of entertainment at a premium up here.

I swung around and turned in close to the north shore. Forest primeval along there, so thickly grown that you couldn't see more than a few yards into the jungly green shadows. Some of the pines overhung the water; the shoreline and a series of narrow inlets where the watershed creeks emptied into the lake were matted with ferns, weeds, snarled roots, collections of dead brush and decaying vegetable matter. The fishing would probably be pretty good in the deeper inlets. So would the kind of beer-for-breakfast, sin-contemplating morning Hal Cantrell had had for himself. Maybe I'd try some of that lazy-man's style of angling myself later in the week.

I was about halfway to Judson's, more or less directly opposite the Dixon and Zaleski cabins, putt-putting along at a couple of knots, when the Johnson quit on me.

No warning; it was running well enough, if a little wheezy, and then all of a sudden it wasn't running at all and the skiff was adrift on the current. I yanked the starter rope. Nothing but a noise that sounded like a death rattle. Fine, dandy. I jerked the rope again, and again, and kept on pulling it until my arm got tired. Then I sat there wasting my breath on a string of not very original oaths, as if the thing were alive and had ancestors. Then I just sat there, sweating in the hot sun, looking at the battered old oars in the bottom. Assuming they didn't fall apart in my hands when I picked them up, I'd have a third of a mile of rowing while the sun broiled my sixty-year-old flesh like a chunk of tough flank steak. It was exertion like that that finished off men my age. Heart attack, stroke, brain aneurysm. Struggling along one second, belly-up the next. Just like the goddamn outboard.

Ahab, hell. Helmsman on the *Titanic* was more like it.

The sun had begun to burn my neck. The skiff was still adrift, moving slowly now, and in so near the overgrown shore that I could almost reach out and touch some of the drooping branches. That gave me an idea. Another inlet was just ahead, part of it in deep shade. I hoisted up the oars — they weren't in quite as bad shape as they looked — and sculled into the inlet and the cool tree shadows. The skeletal arm of a rotting log jutted up from the shore mud; I tied the skiff's painter to it. Then, muttering, I tilted the Johnson out of the water to see if I could figure out what was wrong with it.

Fat chance. My mechanical knowledge is skimpy at best. I lowered it again, made sure the propeller was free of entanglements, and jerked the starter rope. Nothing. Not even a whimper this time. The son of a bitch seemed to have passed beyond the limits of resuscitation and resurrection.

Well?

It was either row and risk the big whopper, or sit here and wait for somebody to rescue me. I didn't care for the second alternative much more than the first. I could chafe my butt for hours on this hard seat before anybody —

Rising noise behind me to the west, engine noise. I looked, and from over that way a bright red skiff was powering in my direction. Nils Ostergaard's skiff. Good old binocular-spying, trouble-sniffing Nils Ostergaard.

He approached at a fast clip, slewed around broadside and cut power just before he reached me — creating a series of wavelets that rocked my boat and made me grab on to the gunwales with both hands. The thought occurred to me that he'd done it on purpose, a gesture of disdain for urbanites who got themselves lost, stranded, or otherwise inconvenienced mountain dwellers like him. I didn't mind. I figured I deserved his scorn, even though this particular predicament wasn't really my fault.

He called out as he maneuvered alongside, "She just quit on you? Won't start again?"

"Dead as a doornail."

"Nope," he said.

"Nope?"

"Ain't dead. Just up to her old tricks. I'll have her up on her feet again in a couple of minutes."

His skiff bumped gently against Zaleski's, prow to stern. He told me to hold us steady, and when I obeyed he took a screwdriver from one of his vest pockets, then leaned over and tilted the Johnson out of the water.

"Watch what I do," he said.

I watched while he removed a section of housing, poked around inside — a process that took just about two minutes. When he tilted the engine back into the water and pulled the rope, the thing coughed once and rebirthed into its old wheezing self.

"Now you know what to do next time it happens."

"Next time?" I said.

"Crotchety bugger, that Johnson. I told Tom Zaleski he ought to get himself a new outboard, but he's too cheap. Rich shyster like him and he won't even spend a hundred fifty bucks for a rebuilt motor. Lawyers," Ostergaard said, and shook his head.

"You mean you've had to fix this thing before?"

"First time it happened to Zaleski. He took care of it himself after that."

"So it happens all the time. Just quits on you."

"Not every time you take her out, maybe. But often enough."

"Why didn't you tell me that yesterday?"

He gave me a look. "Didn't know you had permission to take her out."

"Well, thanks for the help, Nils. And the lesson."

"Couldn't just leave you stranded over here," he said gruffly. "And if you'd tried to row across in this hot sun, hell, you might've had a heart attack or something.

Overweight fellow like you."

"Yeah," I said.

"You going to finish exploring the lake now?"

"Uh-uh. Back to the cabin."

"Take this screwdriver anyway, just in case. You can give it back to me later. Zaleski's got one around there somewhere you can stick in the boat."

"Thanks. You won't need to rescue me again."

"Better not. First time's free, second time costs you dear."

He paused, as if debating something with himself. Then he said, "Be around tonight, will you? At the cabin?"

"Until seven. Then I'm invited to dinner at the Dixons'. Why?"

"Might stop by for a few minutes before or after. Have a beer or two."

"Sure thing. Something on your mind, Nils?"

"Something. Not sure yet what it means."

"What what means?"

"Don't want to say until I check around some."

"I don't follow that."

He paused again. "I think maybe one of the other first-timers ain't what he seems to be."

"What makes you think that?"

"My eyes, for one. Gut feeling, for another."

"What is he, then, if not a fisherman?"

"Not sure about that, either."

"Well, which one is it?"

"Better not say until I check around. Then could be we'll have something to discuss." He shoved his skiff away from mine. "Don't forget about that screwdriver. Mine or Zaleski's."

"I won't."

He waggled a hand, used a short paddle to get himself pointed lakeward, fired up his engine, and went roaring off in the general direction of his cabin. I set off at a much more sedate clip, heading home sadder and wiser and wondering just what Ostergaard had meant by "one of the first-timers ain't what he seems to be."

Midafternoon, just past five Texas time, I tried the Houston Center Marriott again and this time I caught Kerry in her room. She'd tried me twice, she said, and it was a good thing I'd called when I had because she and Jim Carpenter had been invited back to Milo Fisher's ranch for an intimate dinner and they were being picked up by Milo's limo driver at five-thirty.

"A limo, no less. My, my. What does 'intimate dinner' mean, exactly?"

"Don't be jealous, you. All it means is Milo and his wife, Jim and me, and one or two other couples."

"Couples. Uh-huh."

"You *are* jealous. And after you swore up and down —"

"I'm pulling your leg. Yesterday was the big barbecue, right?"

"Yes, and it was fun. There were at least sixty people — friends, neighbors, business associates — and enough food and liquor for a hundred more."

"Sounds like you're winning Fisher over to the Bates and Carpenter team."

"I think we are. I think he'll actually sign with us before we leave Houston. Keep your fingers crossed."

"You betcha."

She asked about Deep Mountain Lake and my vacation so far. I provided a quick report, deemphasizing both the fish episode this morning and my difficulties with Zaleski's cranky outboard this afternoon. After which I steered the conversation back to Milo Fisher, for no reason other than it struck me as a more interesting topic.

"Tell me about this ranch of his," I said. "How big is it?"

"A little less than two thousand acres."

"Two *thousand?*"

"That's not so big by Texas standards. It's quite a showplace. If I ever have to fly back here, I'd like you to come along. You'd love it."

"That's debatable."

"No, you really would. Milo, too."

"I could never love anybody named Milo."

"Like him, I mean. He's a character."

"How so?"

"Oh, you know, stereotypical Texas bombast in the way he dresses and talks. Ten-gallon hats and fancy boots, the whole bit. But it's all a put-on. He's smart and shrewd, and one of the funniest people I've ever met."

"Funny, huh?"

"One joke after another, more one-liners than a stand-up comic. He had everybody in stitches yesterday."

"Dirty jokes, no doubt."

"Not really. His funniest are so clean he could tell them on the Disney Channel."

"For example?"

"There were so many I can remember only a couple. I'll tell you when I see you."

"Tell me one now. I can use a good laugh."

"Well . . . my favorite, then." She chuckled in anticipation, stopped herself, and said, "All right. A married man goes out into the forest, into the deepest part, and while he's there a tree falls. He hears it loud and clear. But he's completely alone — no wife, no other woman within a hundred miles. Is he still wrong?"

I waited.

Silence from her end, so I said, "Go ahead."

"Go ahead?"

"With the rest of the story. I'm listening."

"You don't get it," she said.

"Get it? Get what?"

"The joke."

"I haven't heard the rest of it yet."

"There isn't any more. That's it, that's the joke."

"You mean 'Is he still wrong?' is the punch line?"

"Of *course* it's the punch line. You really don't get it?"

"No, I really don't. What's the point?"

"The point," she said in that tone she uses when her patience is being tried, "is that it's funny. Women think it's hysterical. Most men find it funny, too."

"What's funny about 'Is he still wrong?' "

"The man hears the tree fall, but since

there's no woman around . . . Oh, never mind. Forget it. Forget the whole thing."

"I don't want to forget it. I want to know what it means."

"It's a take-off on the old argument about a tree falling in the woods and does it make a sound if there's nobody around to hear it —"

"I got that part," I said, "the take-off part. But you said the man's there in the forest and *he* hears it fall. Right?"

She said something that sounded like "Gnrrr."

"But his wife's not there, no woman's around, so is he still wrong. That doesn't make any sense. That's the part I don't get."

"For God's sake!" she said. "It's a joke about men and women . . . about marriage and the differences between the sexes. All right, it's stereotypical but that's what makes it so funny, don't you see that? The male-female, husband-wife stereotypes? Like Milo being a Texas stereotype?"

I had no idea what she was talking about. "I don't have any idea what you're talking about," I said.

Silence. A long silence.

"Kerry?"

"You are the most literal, exasperating man I've ever known," she said. "Sometimes I feel like strangling you."

"Because I don't understand some damn stupid joke that doesn't make any sense? A joke is supposed to be funny. It's supposed to have a punch line that makes you laugh."

"We haven't been married long enough," she said. Through her teeth, the way it sounded. "Maybe that's the problem here."

"We haven't been married long enough for what?"

"You'll find out. And when you do, you'll be just like that man in the forest, *you'll still be wrong!*"

I sat there for five minutes after we rang off, and I still didn't get the damn joke.

Wrong about *what?*

Pan-barbecued trout was not quite as good as the pan-fried-in-butter variety, in my opinion, but that didn't stop me from eating two of the large fillets Marian prepared. Chuck had had a profitable morning at his secret fishing hole: a pair of rainbows weighing a total of three and a half pounds. He ate two fillets himself, and we managed to consume most of the salad and potatoes and biscuits that went with them. Personal tastes aside, it was a fine meal served on the Dixons' deck under a sunset sky streaked with burnt orange.

I stayed until nine-thirty, at which point sleepiness and Chuck's insistence that we leave for our outing at the crack of dawn prodded me back to the Zaleski cabin. It wasn't until I was in bed a while later that I remembered my conversation with Nils Ostergaard on the lake.

He hadn't stopped by before dinner and there'd been no sign of him during or after. And even if I'd still been up with the lights on, it was too late now to come calling. Changed his mind about confiding in me, I thought, or put it off until later. His "checking around" must not have produced any results after all.

FROM THE NOTEBOOKS OF
DONALD MICHAEL LATIMER

Sun., June 30 — 9:00 P.M.

Kathryn.

Last night I dreamed about her. This morning I thought about her as I was fishing. This afternoon, when I paid Judson for gas from my dwindling supply of cash, I imagined again what she'll look like when she opens her special gift and how good I'll feel when she's finally dead. Even better than I'll feel when Dixon is finally dead.

Kathryn, Kathryn, Kathryn.

Dead, dead, dead.

I'm down to a little less than $200. I'll have to get a job soon, some damn menial job, but not until after I deliver Kathryn's surprise package to her in Indiana. First things first. Conserve my cash, meanwhile. I won't steal if I do run out, that's one thing I won't do. I'm not a thief. Nobody will ever be able to accuse Donald Michael Latimer of being a common thief.

$3500 gone just like that. But what choice did I have? I needed wheels when they let me out of that hellhole prison, I needed all the tools and components for the bombs, destructive devices, boobytraps, I needed a roof over my head in the Bay Area and this place up here. Necessary expenses, all part of the Plan. $3500 for a hunk of secondhand Detroit crap that keeps overheating, inferior tools and goods instead of the quality material I had to work with in the Army, a drafty shack on the coast that ought to be blown up instead of rented out. Even this cabin is pisspoor compared to the luxury accommodations Kathryn and I shared in the old days. Gone, all gone, the good times and the easy life. And all because of her, what *she* started with her hot pants and her lying, vindictive ways.

A wonder I had any money left after my lawyer and Kathryn and her shyster and all the creditors got done slicing up my assets. $3500 was what they left me, and they'd have got that, too, if I hadn't hidden the cash in the private safe-deposit box while I was out on bail. On top of the world one day, successful business, financial security, nice home, good clothes, a Porsche to drive, what I thought was a rock-solid marriage, and then she brought it all crashing down around my ears. Bitch! Screwing that lousy big-eared pharmacist and then when I caught her, telling me it was *my* fault because she was starved for love and affection. Siccing the cops on me, filing the assault charge after I smacked her, then walking out on me and straight into Lover Boy's scrawny arms. I had a *right* to do what I did to them. I had a right to do a hell of a lot more.

Ah, but not according to the law. Not according to Cotter and Turnbull and Dixon and the California penal code. They picked up where Kathryn left off, persecuted me and took away my freedom, the only thing I had left. Well, now they're the ones who've lost everything. Justice, by God. As ye sow, so shall ye reap, and the bastards sowed the seeds of their own destruction, the lot of them.

Maybe I'll make a few others pay, too, when I'm done with Kathryn and I've saved up enough money. Come back to the Bay Area and send a package to that lawyer of hers, what was his name? Benedict? Snotty, self-righteous prick. Benedict fucking Arnold. And that fat cop who arrested me after the device blew the ass end off Lover Boy's house, the one who treated me like dirt. And my old banker buddy Art Whittington who wouldn't give me a loan, not even a small one, so I could pry myself out of debt. Made that son of a bitch thousands in mutual fund investments, and a cold shoulder was the thanks I got. *They* deserve a payback, too. So do all the others, business associates and fair-weather friends, everybody who deserted me before and after the trial, left me to endure five years of torment alone. Make little presents for each of them, boom boom boom boom boom!

Kathryn first, though.

Kathryn next.

Might as well start assembling her present while I'm waiting for Dixon to show up and claim his. I've done enough savoring, the way you savor sleeping with a woman for the first time. Now I'm ready for the preparations, the foreplay to the Big B. I have all the components except for the last one, and I can get that from any butcher shop on the way to Lawler Bluffs, IN. I brought everything in from the car Friday night, after dark, when I was sure nobody was around. Tool kit and the carton from the supermarket Dumpster in Half Moon Bay and the bag of bubble wrap and the microswitch and the black powder. And the jar of marbles, of course. It's sitting right here on the table in front of me as I write. Glass marbles, different kinds, different colors, all very pretty, like eyes winking at me in the light from the desk lamp.

Those marbles were an inspiration. All the thought I gave to what to put in Kathryn's surprise, something just for her — never mind the pharmacist and their brat, they're incidental. Couldn't make up my mind, and then as soon as I saw the marbles in the toy store window I knew they were perfect, I knew exactly what else to get, too.

She took everything from me, she got all the marbles. Okay, then, I'll give her two hundred more than she bargained for, two hundred cheap glass marbles that'll fly apart in a million fragments from the force of the blast and rip her rotten flesh to shreds.

Second thing you give an unfaithful bitch for her final sendoff? Why, a bagful of rancid bones, naturally. Soup bones that'll splinter and gouge and tear the same as the marbles.

So long, Kathryn. Rest in pieces.

Too bad I can't tell her beforehand what she'll be getting. Too bad she'll never know. Always accusing me of not having a sense of humor. Well, this proves different, doesn't it? Proves I've got a terrific sense of humor.

She'll get a bang out of her present, all right.

And then I'll have the last laugh.

I just reread the previous page, the line about rest in pieces and the lines about her getting a bang out of her present and me having the last laugh. They started me chuckling, then roaring until my belly hurt. Now I've got the hiccups. I think I'd better

Somebody's at the door.

Knock knock. Knock knock.

Who the hell can that be at this hour?

7

When Chuck showed up in the morning — or the middle of the night, depending on your point of view — the sky was still dark except for a faint phosphorescence on the eastern horizon and I was working on my second cup of coffee and just starting to come alive. Ungodly hour to be up. Two mornings in a row now I'd been out of bed before daylight, and that was at least one too many. Tomorrow I'd sleep until nine in deference to my old bones.

"All set?" he asked eagerly. "Man, I can't wait to get going."

"Me, either," I lied. "Just let me finish my coffee."

"I've got a Thermosful. From the pot Mom made last night."

I tried not to grimace. Marian's coffee was strong enough fresh-brewed. By now, last night's batch ought to be as chewy as black tar.

"We'll take our boat, okay?" Chuck said.

"Boat? I thought we were heading into the woods."

"We are. But you have to take a boat to

get to where you can hike to Chuck's Hole."

"Chuck's Hole, huh?"

"Yeah. I found it, so I named it after myself."

"Good for you. How much of a hike is it?"

"Not much. Come on, we want to get there before sunup."

I asked him what kind of flies I ought to take, bowing to his expertise. He looked through my case, pointed out half a dozen that I transferred into the plastic pocket case. Then I gathered my rod and creel and followed him out and over to the Dixon property.

He did the piloting, angling their skiff out across the lake to the northwest. I sat on the prow seat and slugged black-tar coffee from his Thermos. Terrible stuff, but it did ward off the pre-dawn chill and get the rest of my juices flowing. By the time we reached one of the narrow inlets on the far shore I was more or less alert, even starting to feel a little of the boy's enthusiasm.

Once we entered the inlet he shut off the outboard, lifted it out of the water to protect the propeller from snags, then used an oar to pole us along. The way ahead seemed impassable, a black wall of tree branches and undergrowth. But after we struggled through the first tangle, me keeping my head down at Chuck's direction, we were onto a quick stream that appeared to be several yards wide and deep enough so that the skiff's bottom didn't scrape its rocky bed. Chuck poled us upstream for a hundred yards or so, through a series of twists and turns. It was dark in there, even with the sky beginning to take on dawn light visible in patches through the overhead branches — so dark it was like drifting in a wilderness maze at midnight. The air was moist, cold, heavy with the smells of fresh and stagnant water, growing and rotting vegetation. Frogs stopped their croaking as we passed, commenced again behind us. My face and neck became a feeding ground for a kamikaze legion of mosquitoes; the more I squashed, the more showed up in buzzing, diving assaults.

"How much farther?" I asked.

"We're almost to where we leave the boat. It's neat in here, huh?"

"Neat," I said, and whacked another mosquito.

Pretty soon the terrain humped and the stream widened into what looked to be a pool at the foot of a series of short, naturally terraced steps. The water came bubbling down over them, making cheerful noises in the gloomy stillness. That was as far as we could take the boat — unless we portaged up over the rise, and Chuck relieved me of that unappealing idea by announcing, as he nosed us onto a slope of shore mud, that we'd hike the rest of the way.

"It's not far," he said. "About half a mile."

"What about this pool right here? No good?"

"Nah," he said. "Chuck's Hole is where they hang out."

So we tromped overland on an all but invisible deer trail, Chuck setting a brisk pace despite the poor light and me struggling to keep up and not injure myself on rocks, root tangles, and other obstacles. It wasn't really a bad trek, even though it was mostly uphill in a series of gradual rises, but by its end I was tired, scratched, lumpy with mosquito bites, and wondering why I put myself through little adventures like this. For the kid's sake, in this case — sure. But part of it, too, maybe, was to prove to myself that I was not quite to the geezer-in-the-porch-rocker stage yet.

Yeah, I thought, except that right now that porch rocker looks pretty good. Eh, Grandpappy?

Where we emerged, finally, was into a big, open glade filled with early-morning light.

The sky was a milky blue that would deepen and brighten as the sun rose. The creek ran off to the left and the pool there, shaded by trees and a mossy outcrop, was long and wide and pretty as the proverbial postcard. As soon as I saw it, I felt less creaky and more pleased with my surroundings.

"Chuck's Hole," he said proudly.

"I'm impressed. No kidding."

He grinned. "Best place to fish is up on that outcrop."

"You're the boss."

He led the way upstream to a place above the pool where we could ford it, then back to the outcrop. He already had a line in the water by the time I finished tying on one of my flies, a #14 Iron Blue Dun. Chuck was using his prized PMD, the #18 Mathews Sparkle Dun with the Zelon shuck. It must've been right for this pool because he got the first couple of nibbles, hooked and then lost a smallish brown, hooked and landed the first fish of the day, a handsome speckled cutthroat in the pound-and-a-half range.

We'd been there about forty minutes before I had any luck. I made a pretty fair cast into the shadows under a thick cluster of ferns and snaky tree roots, and almost immediately something smacked the fly and jerked the line taut, with enough force to yank the rod out of my hand if I hadn't had a tight grip on the butt. I knew I'd hooked a rainbow even before I saw it, by the way it battled: a cutthroat brown is tricky and fights with its head, while a rainbow is stronger, speedier, and fights with its tail. It took me a while to work the fish and reel him in, with Chuck calling excited encouragement the entire time. He'd brought a net and he used it when I lifted the flopping trout out of the water. Otherwise I might've lost it — and before long I wished I had.

"A beauty," the boy said, his eyes shining. "Two pounds at least, maybe two and a half. Nice going, man!"

I removed the hook from the rainbow's mouth. As soon as it was free, blood glistening on the barbed tip, the same aversion as yesterday came over me: I didn't want to kill it. I think I would have released it, the way I had the cutthroat brown, if Chuck hadn't been there grinning approval at me. We'd forged a bond this morning, the boy and me, become friends across the double-wide generation gap; if I let the trout go, I knew he would lose respect for me, no matter what I said to justify it. He was only twelve and fishing was his passion; he'd never understand. I weighed his disfavor against the fish's life. And the fish lost. The arguments on the side of my relationship with Chuck were stronger: The whole purpose of this outing was to catch trout for eating, wasn't it? I'd had no compunction about the trout I'd eaten last night, had I? Or about killing and consuming hundreds of other fish over the past forty-some years? Why spoil things for Chuck because I'd suddenly developed a problem? A fish, for Christ's sake. As Strayhorn had said, it was just a fish.

None of that helped much. I still did not want to destroy the rainbow, and if I turned the job over to Chuck it would be the coward's way out. I'm a lot of things, but a coward isn't one of them. So I used the handle of my knife, doing it quickly, then gave the stilled body to the boy to put in his creel with the one he'd caught. He didn't mind that; he considered it a gesture of our friendship.

"I'm going to take a break," I said, "finish the rest of the coffee. You go ahead and keep your line out."

"Sure," he said. "Plenty more down there. Bet I catch a bigger one than yours."

"Bet you do, too."

I moved off the outcrop and sat in the shade, my back against a pine bole. I felt

125

lousy for a time, worse than the situation warranted, but then I began to develop a different perspective on what had just happened. Suppose, I thought, I'd killed the trout not for Chuck's sake or the sake of my relationship with him, but for my own sake. To prove something to myself, beyond any doubt.

That I was through with fishing? Maybe. No, probably. There was still pleasure for me in tramping the woods, picking out a suitable spot, casting a line, but the affinity for the catch, the fight, the final victory was all but gone. Finishing off that big, strong rainbow, then, might've been a symbolic act of closure: washing my hands of the sport in the trout's blood.

But there was more to it than that. It wasn't just the prospect of sacrificing any more fish that left me cold; it was a visceral repugnance at the idea of ever killing *anything* again.

So damned much death in my sixty years. All the corpses I'd seen, all the atrocities one human being can visit upon another. My own direct responsibility for one man's sudden end, and indirect responsibility for a couple of others'. The countless other life forms that had ceased to exist because of me, too: the birds I'd felled with a slingshot when I was a kid, the buck I'd shot and wounded and had to put out of its misery on my one and only hunting trip, all the trout and bass and salmon I'd caught, all the rodents and even the insects like those mosquitoes this morning that I'd carelessly disposed of. Enough. I'd had enough.

Life is too short, too precious. Even to a fish. Even to a bug. And man's intelligence puts him well atop the natural food chain; no creature has the right to interrupt his cycle of life, especially one of his own kind. So why should he maintain the smug, arrogant position that it's okay for him to indulge in casual slaughter outside his species?

Let others rationalize answers to that question. Not me. Not anymore.

"Hey, look!" Chuck called above the throb of the Evinrude outboard. "Something's goin' on over at the Stapletons'."

I looked toward where he was pointing. We were two-thirds of the way across the lake, heading for home, and the distance was too great for me to make out much except that half a dozen people were clustered behind one of the alpine cottages halfway between Judson's and the Dixon cabin.

I called back to Chuck, "Who're the Stapletons?"

"Family from Reno. But they're not here yet, they don't come up until July."

"Cottage closed up, then?"

"Yeah. Maybe somebody busted in or something. Stole their padlocks like they stole ours."

"The gang of padlock thieves."

"Right. Let's go see what's up, okay?"

"You've got the tiller."

He changed course, pointing us toward the Stapleton property. It was midmorning now and warm on the lake, the sky cloud-streaked. The boy had wanted to stay at Chuck's Hole and fish a while longer, but I'd talked him out of it, pleading hunger and promising him a pancake breakfast at Judson's. He'd caught two more trout, a cutthroat and a rainbow marginally larger than mine. He was so pleased with his morning's take and the fact that he'd been able to make good on his boast that he hadn't been bothered by having to fish alone. I'd lied about there being something wrong with my rod, a minute crack in the bamboo, to explain my unwillingness to join him. The truth would only have bewildered him. It was my truth anyway, not his.

As we neared the Stapletons', the shore

group separated into recognizable individuals. Mack Judson, Fred Dyce, Jacob Strayhorn, two of the summer residents I'd met at the cafe, and one man I didn't know. When Judson saw that we were heading in their direction, he hurried onto the dock, making stay-away gestures with both hands. The others hung back on shore.

Chuck ignored the gestures. I was about to warn him off myself, but we were close enough now so that I could see something else on the property — a tarpaulin spread out in front of a lean-to filled with stacks of firewood. The humped shape of what lay under the tarp made my stomach turn over. I didn't say anything to Chuck. I didn't let myself think anything yet, either.

The boy cut power and nosed us in to the float below where Judson was standing, a bleak frown on his craggy face. But the frown wasn't for us; we were nothing more to him than a distraction. He called down to Chuck, "Why didn't you mind me, boy? This is no place for you now."

"Why? What's going on?"

"Been an accident. A bad one."

"What kind of accident?"

"Nils Ostergaard. He's dead."

"Dead? Mr. Ostergaard is *dead?*"

"Since some time last night."

Death on my mind all morning and now this.
I lifted myself out of the skiff, climbed a
ramp that led from the float onto the dock.
"What happened, Mack?"

"Nils went out about seven last night and
didn't come back," Judson said. "Sometimes he'd stray off and stay out late, so
Callie wasn't worried when she went to bed
about eleven. His wife, Callie. Plenty worried when she woke up this morning and he
still wasn't home. Came and told me and I
got up a search party."

"How long ago'd you find him?"

"About twenty minutes. Took us a couple
of hours of hunting. His pickup was in some
trees near the resort, so we searched there
first. That's why it took so long."

"How'd he die?"

Dyce and the man I didn't know had wandered out onto the dock. They heard my
question, and Dyce said, "Cracked skull.
Harper here and me're the ones who found
him." The sullen belligerence was absent
today; he seemed subdued. Maybe the presence of death had humbled him a little.

"Poking around in the dark, seems like,"
Judson said, "and tripped and fell against
that stack of cordwood up there. Split his
head open on a log."

"Why would he be poking around a de-

130

serted cottage in the dark?"

"That was the way he was. Self-appointed watchdog. Must've seen or heard something, decided to take a look."

I said, thinking out loud, "Funny he'd leave his pickup such a long way off."

"Not if you knew Nils. No telling what he was liable to do, or why."

"Are you sure it was an accident?"

They all looked at me. Strayhorn was there, too, by then; so was Hal Cantrell, who'd appeared from up on the road and followed him onto the dock. Strayhorn smiled his small, pale smile and said, "Don't you think it was?"

"I didn't say that."

"Then why ask the question?"

"He's a cop," Dyce said. "They're all suspicious."

I had nothing to say to that.

Strayhorn said, "Why don't you have a look at the body, judge for yourself?"

"Not my place to do that."

"County law's on the way," the man named Harper said. "Be here with an ambulance any minute."

"Take a look anyway," Strayhorn said to me. "See what you think. I'd be interested to know."

"Why?"

131

He made that shrugging movement with his head. "Curiosity. Can't hurt to take a look, can it?"

"Sure," Cantrell said, "take a look. Why not?"

I glanced at Judson; he lifted his shoulders, let them fall. He was too upset to care one way or the other. "Go ahead if you want."

No, I thought. Better keep out of it.

"Come on," Strayhorn said, "you've seen dead men before." Challenging me, the way he had at Two Creek Bar. Why? He didn't like me, that was plain enough. Because I'd released the cutthroat brown and then laughed about it? Something skewed in him, if that was the reason.

"All right," I said, to shut him up and keep it from becoming an issue. I glanced down at a pale-faced Chuck in the skiff. "Go on back to your cabin. I'll walk from here."

"But I want to be here when —"

"Go on, Chuck. Your mother should know about this. Go home and tell her."

He didn't argue, and as I moved away, following Judson and the others, I heard the Evinrude crank up. Give a kid something important to do and he'll do it — and there's nothing so important as the bearing

132

of bad news. If that wasn't true, the world media would shut down and every journalist of every kind would be out of a job.

It was Judson who lifted the tarp so I could see what was left of Nils Ostergaard. My stomach kicked again; no matter how many times you face sudden death there's always the same involuntary physical reaction, the same mixture of sadness and revulsion. The wound was on the left side of the head, dried blood from the ear up over the temple. Ants and other insects had been at the blood; there were still a few of them moving around. A piece of bark clung there, too, evidently from the log that had been dislodged from the lean-to pile and lay near his head. Smears of dried blood stained the log as well.

"So what do you think?" Cantrell asked.

I took the tarp from Judson without answering, drew it back off the body. Ostergaard wore a plaid lumberman's jacket, a blue shirt, a pair of faded Levi's. Nothing bulky in any of the pockets, nothing on the ground around him, and both his hands were empty.

"No flashlight," I said.

Dyce said, "Flashlight?"

"Why would he leave his car in some trees several hundred yards away and then walk back down here without a flashlight?"

"He didn't need one. Bright sky last night."

"Not so bright here. Lot of shadowed ground."

Judson said, "Nils knew each property like the back of his hand. He didn't need a light to find his way around, even as old as he was. What's the damn point of all this talk?"

"The point," Strayhorn said, "is that he didn't find his way around so well last night." His gaze settled on me once more. "Right?"

I ignored him again and asked Judson, "Did you check the cottage to see if it's secure?"

"We checked it. Locked up tight."

"The outbuildings?"

"Same."

"No signs of trespassing?"

"No. None."

"Cops," Dyce said. Some of his snotty sullenness had returned. "Jesus Christ. The old guy fell down and hit his head and killed himself. Period, end of story."

"But you don't think so," Strayhorn said to me.

"Did I say I didn't think so?"

"You seem to have doubts."

134

"No doubts," I lied. "It was an accident, just as Dyce says. That's pretty obvious."

"So you're satisfied."

"I'm satisfied. Aren't you?"

Either that comeback put an end to his little game, or he tired of it; in any case, he shut up and drifted into the background, the way he had in the cafe on Saturday evening. None of us had any more to say. We were seven men alone with our own thoughts, like mourners at a grave site, when the sheriff's deputies and an ambulance arrived from Quincy five minutes later.

8

The whole thing felt wrong to me.

It felt manipulated, arranged. It felt like homicide.

In my mind's ear I kept hearing Nils Ostergaard's words to me on the lake yesterday: *I think maybe one of the other first-timers ain't what he seems to be.* Connection? If it was a homicide, that was the most likely angle. Who else would have a reason to kill a proddy but harmless old man like Ostergaard and then try to make it look like an accident?

But what motive would a man who wasn't what he seemed to be have? Something that involved those missing padlocks on the Dixon property, maybe? Or was that stretching things too far?

And what was this guy and why was he at Deep Mountain Lake if he wasn't a fisherman?

None of it added up to anything but wild speculation. Which was the main reason I hadn't voiced any of my reservations or suspicions to the sheriff's deputies. There were ordinary explanations for Ostergaard leaving his pickup where he had, for him not taking his flashlight and skulking around in the dark. The wound on his temple had looked to be deep and long, more in keeping with a bludgeoning than a fall; but with all the dried blood I couldn't be sure of the dimensions, and, besides, I was no forensics expert and an old man's flesh is thin, his bones brittle. A fall *could* have done the damage.

I told myself, as I walked away from the Stapleton property, that I ought to just forget it, let the county authorities handle it as they saw fit. None of my business, was it? Except that it was, in a way. Ostergaard had been planning to confide in me — involve me in whatever he'd nosed up. By the same token, his death had passed the gauntlet on to me. There were other arguments, too: It had been pretty obvious from the way the deputies talked and acted that there wouldn't be much of an investigation, if any at all; accidental death would almost certainly be the official verdict. And I could not shake the feeling of wrongness, or the sense of obligation it carried. If Ostergaard had been murdered, I owed it to him and his widow to try to prove it. *Once a cop, always a cop,* he'd said to me. Right, and good cops look out for their own and do what they can to uphold the principles of duty and justice. Those principles don't seem to mean as much nowadays as they once did, but they mattered to me and they'd mattered to the man I believed Ostergaard had been.

Talking myself into it was what I was doing. Not that I needed much convincing.

Too much death on my mind today. That worried me a little, that I might be developing a preoccupation with it. But you can't be confronted by death and not have it affect you in some way. An emotional empath like me couldn't, anyway. Besides, there are different kinds of death and dying, the explicable and the inexplicable. I'd come up against both this morning, one right after the other, and it was the second kind, not the first, that kept troubling me. If I had a preoccupation, it was the same one I'd always had, the one that had motivated me for fifty-some years: an obsessive involvement with life and the need to solve at least a few of its mysteries.

The last cottage on the western shore was a green clapboard affair with a steep alpine roof; a burnt wood sign at the foot of the drive said *The Ostergaards* in Spencerian script. A dark blue van was parked near the front door, which I took to mean that Callie

Ostergaard was still here. I'd half expected to find the place locked up, the widow gone away to Quincy to be with family or friends.

An older woman with hennaed hair and a take-charge manner came out to meet me as I climbed from the car. Not Callie Ostergaard; one of the summer residents, who announced that she was staying with Mrs. Ostergaard until her daughter arrived from someplace called Graeagle. I identified myself and asked how the widow was bearing up.

"As well as can be expected," the woman said. "She's a very strong person, thank God."

"I'm sure she is. I'd like to speak to her, if I could."

"Well, I don't know. . . ."

"Would you ask her if she'd mind seeing me? Just briefly? I have a few questions that might be important."

"Questions? About what happened to Nils?"

"Please ask her."

". . . All right. You wait here."

I waited about a minute. Then the door opened again and the woman motioned me inside, led me along a central hallway that emptied into a large lakefront room. Dark and cool in there: the drapes had been drawn. The woman sitting in one of two matching armchairs was in her seventies, trim, tiny, with short shag-cut white hair and a nut-brown face that seemed smooth, almost wrinkle-free in the half light.

"I'm sorry to intrude, Mrs. Ostergaard —"

"Not at all. It was good of you to come by." Strong voice, with just an undercurrent of the grief she must be feeling. If she'd done any crying, it was long finished; she had her public face on, the one that a woman in a time of crisis applies with lipstick and rouge and an effort of will. "June said you have questions?"

I glanced at the henna-haired woman. She understood what the glance meant; her eyes shifted to Callie Ostergaard, who smiled wanly and said, "It's all right, dear." No argument from June; she nodded and left us alone.

Mrs. Ostergaard invited me to sit down. When I'd done that, she said, "Nils spoke well of you. He doesn't . . . didn't always care for strangers."

"I liked him, too. I'm really very sorry."

"Thank you. It's so hard to believe he's gone, that I'll never hear his voice again. It hasn't really sunk in yet. I expect him to walk in the door any second. . . ." Her head moved: a sad and bewildered little negative. "We were married fifty-seven years, you know. My father, the old coot, said it wouldn't last six months."

"Mrs. Ostergaard —"

"Callie. Everyone calls me Callie."

"Callie, did Nils tell you where he was going last night? What his plans were?"

"No. No, he didn't. He often went off by himself at night. On patrol, he called it. It gave him something to do that made him feel useful."

"Did he mention the Stapleton property?"

"Not that I recall."

"Does it seem odd to you that he'd park his truck off the road and go patrolling on foot, without a flashlight?"

"Odd? Well, he might have seen or heard something that made him suspicious. All sorts of things made Nils suspicious, not always with good cause."

"Such as one of this year's first-time visitors?"

". . . I don't know what you mean."

I related my conversation with Nils on the lake. "Did he say anything to you along those lines?"

Small headshake. "He could be secretive, Nils could. Fifty-seven years, and still he kept his little secrets."

"Do you have any idea what he meant by a fisherman not being what he seemed to be?"

"A criminal of some kind, I suppose. Hiding out."

"Why would a criminal come to Deep Mountain Lake to hide out?"

"I can't imagine that one would. But Nils . . . well, all his years in law enforcement were uneventful. He never once used his gun, you know. He wouldn't admit it, but I think he always dreamed of capturing a wanted man, a dangerous fugitive. Being a hero." She blinked rapidly several times as she spoke the last. If it was a struggle against a new rush of tears, she won it with an effort. "Foolish. He was always a hero to me."

Those words weren't really for my ears; they were a verbalization of what she was feeling inside. I let a few seconds pass before I said, "There are four first-timers here now, Callie, including me. Did Nils say anything to you about the others, in any context?"

"I'm sorry, my mind isn't clear. What are their names?"

"Jacob Strayhorn is one."

"Strayhorn. Yes, I met him. Strange man. Like the little boy who pulled wings off flies, grown up. Nils said he wouldn't trust that man as far as he could throw him."

"Was there any specific reason he said that?"

"Strayhorn's eyes. Something about his eyes."

I said, "Hal Cantrell? He's another."

Her lips moved, repeating the name silently to herself. "I don't know him," she said at length. "At least, I don't remember the name."

"Real estate broker from Pacifica. Talkative and sly, but friendly enough."

"I don't believe I've met him. Or that Nils mentioned his name. But my memory . . ."

"I understand. Dyce, Fred Dyce?"

"Oh, yes, the surly one. Nils had words with him when he first arrived."

"An argument, you mean?"

"About fishing."

"In general, or — ?"

"He said Dyce was a blowhard who pretended to be an expert but had gotten all his knowledge from books. Nils hated that type of person."

"A man who isn't what he claims to be."

"Well, yes, that's right."

"Did Nils accuse him of it to his face?"

"Oh yes. He never minced words."

"What was Dyce's reaction?"

"The usual with that sort. Bluster and obscenities."

"Were there any other run-ins between them?"

"Not that I know of."

"Did Nils mention Dyce's name yesterday or last night?"

"No." She watched me steadily for a time. "You think that what happened wasn't an accident."

It was a statement, not a question, and it caught me unprepared. I was trying to frame a response when she said, "Don't keep anything from me, please."

"I won't, Callie. The truth is, I don't know. It could've been just that, a tragic accident."

"Mack Judson said there was no doubt of it. The deputies who came by seemed to feel the same. Why don't you agree?"

"No specific reason," I said uncomfortably. "A feeling, that's all. A kind of hunch."

"Suspicious. You're another like Nils."

"I didn't mean to upset you —"

"Upset me? My Lord, if his death wasn't an accident, if that man Dyce or one of the others . . . I want to know it. I *have* to know. Someone has to find out."

I nodded. "Someone will."

"You. That *is* why you came here, isn't it? Why you've been asking so many questions?"

"Not exactly. I'm not in a position to conduct an official investigation."

"Not even if you were hired to?"

"By you, Callie? No. I don't do business that way."

"An unofficial investigation, then. For my sake and for Nils's. You didn't know him well, but he was a good man. A *good* man —"

She broke off at the sound of a car arriving in a hurried squeal of brakes. "That will be Ellen," she said after a moment. "Our daughter. Don't mind her if she carries on. She's very high-strung."

I couldn't think of anything else to say. I sat like a lump as a woman's voice rose querulously out front.

Callie leaned toward me, her eyes fire-bright, and tapped my knee with a bony forefinger. "Find out," she said in a fierce whisper. "Please. Find out!"

FROM THE NOTEBOOKS OF
DONALD MICHAEL LATIMER

Mon., July 1 — 1:30 P.M.

I didn't want to kill the old man. *Last* thing I wanted to happen, somebody to die up here before Dixon shows and pieces of Mr. Prosecutor go flying through the air. But what choice did I have? Damn Osterfart, he didn't even give me a chance to take him out *my* way, with a bomb, destructive device, boobytrap designed for a meddling old bastard like him.

Knock knock, and there he was. Like to talk to you, he said, hard-eyed, mind if I come in?, and before I could say anything, react to stop him, he was inside. Looking around the way cops do, acting like he owned the place. I'd covered up the table before I went to the door, but the jar of marbles, the tools, my notebooks made lumps and shapes and he could see the carton and the bubble wrap on the floor.

What're you building there? he said.

Not building anything, I said.

No? he said, and the way he said it, I knew he'd been snooping around outside, looking through the window. The shade was down, but there might've been just enough of a gap. What's under the sheet? he said.

Trout flies, I said. It was the only thing I could think of. I tie my own flies, I said.

That so? he said. Mind if I have a look?

Rather you didn't, I said. What do you want, I said, this time of night?

His eyes shifted to my binoculars hanging from the back of one of the chairs. Saw you out on the lake, he said, anchored over on the north shore watching cabins through those glasses. On more than one occasion, he said. Seems you spend more time looking than you do fishing, he said.

I tried to bluff him, make him believe he was imagining things. He wouldn't bluff. Shrewd old bugger knew something was up and he'd keep picking at it, picking at it until he found out what it was.

His eyes were back on the lumps and shapes, the carton and bubble wrap. Let's have a look at those flies of yours, he said, and he started over there and I knew I'd have to kill him, right then and there, no dicking around. I picked up a chunk of firewood from the basket and he was just lifting a corner of the sheet, bending forward to look underneath, when I eased up behind him. He never knew what hit him. He pulled the sheet half off the table when he fell, knocked off a screwdriver and the soldering iron, thump, thump, and then the big Thump when *he* landed. A quick look was all I needed. Skull cracked, blood oozing but not for long. One dead Osternosy.

So then I had his scrawny corpse to deal with. Had anybody seen him come here? I took a quick look outside. Nobody around. And I didn't see his pickup. Parked it in those trees where we found it today, cat-footed over here to see what he could see. Ostersneaky.

Back inside I thought it all over carefully, weighing my options. Not good, any way you sliced it. (Sliced options? Hah! You can slice an onion, but you can't slice an option.) Make him disappear completely or make it look like an accident, those were the only two that made any sense. Wait until late, take him out in the woods some-where and bury him, nobody'd ever find his grave except animals and bugs — eas-iest and safest way. But when he turned up missing there'd be search parties, county cops tramping all over the area for days. The more cops and people around, the bigger the hazard to me and the less likely Dixon does what he's supposed to do when he finally hauls his ass up here from the city. Everything has to seem *normal* when he shows, more or less normal anyway.

Accident was the smart way to go, I decided. I wrapped the old bugger's body in the sheet, the bloody chunk of wood in a towel, waited until late, made sure I was alone, carried him out and drove him to the first deserted cottage that had a woodpile, carried him down there and arranged him and laid the bloodstained wood next to his head where it'd look like a piece from the pile, and got the hell out of there. Hard work, sweating like a pig when I got back here and burned the sheet and towel in the fireplace, but worth the effort and the risk.

Handled it all just right, too. Accident. Everybody thinks so, Judson and the others and the sheriff's deputies.

Everybody except that smart-ass private cop?

Him. That one. I was sure he'd buy it along with the rest, and maybe he did, but now I'm not so sure. All those questions he asked, but then he backed off and said he had no doubts it was an accident, but maybe he does have doubts and he's planning to do some snooping of his own. Another one like Osternosy and twice as dangerous if he gets the scent. Deadly enemy — I knew that the first time I laid eyes on him, didn't I? I should have handled him differently, but it's too late to worry about that now. Hindsight, the great teacher.

Ticklish situation. I could take him out, fix up a little surprise for him, boom! I know just how to do it, too — now. But I don't want to risk it before Dixon comes unless I have to. Another dead cop blows the whole game sky high. Dixon, Dixon. *He's* the one who has to blow sky high.

Won't be long. Another day, two at the most. And even if that geriatric Mike Hammer is suspicious and comes snooping around here, so what? Nothing for him to find. All my tools, components, everything — locked away in the car. Put it all in the trunk last night while I was waiting to get rid of the old man's corpse. Cleared up what little blood there was, put the place in apple-pie order.

So let him snoop. Let him ask as many questions as he wants. I know how to deal with him now, one way or the other. No damn private dickhead is going to screw things up for Donald Michael Latimer and his personal and private interpretation of Chapter 3.2, Section 12355, Subdivision (c) of the fucking California Penal Code.

9

I wanted to talk to one or both of the Judsons first, then Fred Dyce, but it was a while before I got to the resort and an even longer while before I got to Dyce. Less than three minutes after I left the Ostergaard cabin I rounded a bend in the road and came on Marian Dixon walking toward me along the shoulder. She stopped when she recognized my car, waited for me to pull up alongside.

"I'm on my way to see Callie," she said. Her eyes were sad, empty of their usual animation. "Mrs. Ostergaard. Is that where you've been?"

I said it was. And that I was sorry I hadn't stopped by and asked her to come along with me but that I'd been distracted.

"It's all right. How is she?"

"Bearing up. Her daughter's with her now. And a woman named June."

"June Adams. Good — Callie shouldn't be alone at a time like this." She brushed strands of hair away from her eyes and cheeks; the wind was up and it immediately blew the hair back across her face, so that she seemed to be looking at me through a screen of tattered yellow silk.

I said, "Hop in. I'll drive you."

Marian came around and slipped in beside me. When I had the car turned and moving in the opposite direction, she said, "I keep having trouble believing Nils is gone. He was such a presence here, such a good friend to everyone."

Except one person, maybe, I thought. But I kept the thought to myself; there was nothing to be gained in sharing my suspicions with anybody other than Callie Ostergaard at this point. Instead, I gave voice to a platitude: "At least his death was quick."

"And relatively painless. I called Rita Judson and she told me what happened." A couple of beats, and then she said, "Thank you for sending Chuck home to tell me."

"I thought it'd be better if he didn't hang around."

"Yes, and I'm grateful."

"He handling it okay? He and Nils seemed pretty fond of each other."

"They were. He wouldn't talk about it, wouldn't come with me to see Callie, just shut himself up in his room. He'll be all right, I think, but I wish Pat was here. He responds more readily to his father than he does to me. The male bond, I suppose."

"Have you talked to Pat yet?"

"Yes. I called his office after I spoke to Rita and he'd just come back from court. He was very upset. He's known Nils ever since he was a boy."

"Does he know yet when he'll be driving up?"

"No. It may not be until Wednesday."

"Anything new on the bombings, did he say?"

"Forensics is nearly finished examining and comparing the evidence from the two crime scenes. They should know whether or not there's a signature match within twenty-four hours."

"That's something, at least."

"Yes. Something."

We were at the Ostergaard cabin; I stopped at the head of the drive to let Marian out. Before she shut the door, she said, "Would you mind if I asked a small favor?"

"Go ahead."

"Could you stop by later and talk to Chuck? He likes and respects you, and you've had so much experience with . . . well, you know. It might be good for him right now."

"Well . . ."

"I don't mean a father-son kind of talk —
Pat will be here soon enough. Just . . . man
to man. But if you'd rather not . . ."

The look on her face made me say, "All
right, I'll give it a try. No promises,
though."

"None expected."

She thanked me, went on down the incline. And I drove away, thinking: Talk,
listen, provide the interim male bond, the
voice of experience with . . . well, you know.
Sure, why not? I was good at that sort of
thing, wasn't I? Large part of the job, wasn't
it? I was not just a skip-tracer, a keyhole
peeper; I was also a priest, a therapist, a
teacher, a grief counselor, all too often a
sin-eater, and yes, by golly, a surrogate pop
now and then. Come one, come all, unload
your woes on me and I'll chew them and
swallow them and regurgitate comfort and
strength and wisdom that'll lighten your
burden, make your life and the lives of your
loved ones easier, more relieved. A spiritual
leader, that was something else I was supposed to be — the wise old charismatic bell-
wether guiding the lost and the hurt and the
damaged and the innocent onto the path of
righteousness, redemption, true under-
standing. Like a poor, pale-imitation Jesus,
with bonded license and .38 Colt Body-

guard instead of rod and staff, with heart full of love and head full of sagacity and belly full of . . . well, you know.

I shook myself, shook away the bitter thoughts. Now where had all that come from? All she'd asked me to do was talk to her son. No, it was more than that — it was a gesture of faith and trust in me, a man she hardly knew, offered as so many others had offered before her. Faith and trust were two names for it; another was shifted responsibility, the kind that I didn't always want and too often didn't deserve because I couldn't live up to it, couldn't be or do any of the things that were expected of me.

Just say no. That was a nice little slogan, the perfect panacea. Too bad I was one of those who had never learned how, even to save my wise old charismatic psyche another bruise or two. The word simply wasn't in my lexicon. Hell, I could not even say no to myself.

Rita Judson was manning — womanning? — the grocery counter when I walked in. Through the archway I could see Mack and a few other men clustered near the bar; I detoured over that way for a better view. They were holding a private wake for Nils, the way it looked, their faces solemn and what conversation there was uttered in low voices. Fred Dyce wasn't among them. Neither were Strayhorn or Cantrell.

I went on to the counter and commiserated with Rita for a minute or so before I asked my questions. Drawing her out about the three other newcomers wasn't difficult; she didn't mind sharing what she knew, though it was not much about any of them. When I left her, this was what I had:

Fred Dyce. He lived in the San Fernando Valley, not L.A. proper — Van Nuys. Sold used cars and drove one himself, a Jeep Cherokee with vanity plates: LKYDYCE. Marital and family status unknown; he wouldn't talk about his personal life. Or explain what had brought him all the way up to Deep Mountain Lake from Southern California. He drank a lot, mostly sour-mash bourbon with beer chasers, but so far he'd kept it and his hostility under control. His cabin was number eight, on the north side lakefront.

Jacob Strayhorn. Born and still lived in Stockton. What he did for a living was uncertain; he'd told Mack that he was in the manufacturing business, but he'd been reticent about what it was he manufactured. Kept to himself and volunteered almost nothing of a personal nature, beyond the fact that he was divorced. Drove the beat-up Chrysler I'd seen on my way to Two Bar Creek yesterday morning. He wasn't staying at the resort; he'd rented one of the smaller private cottages downshore — not far from the Stapleton property.

Hal Cantrell. Real-estate broker in and resident of Pacifica. Married a dozen years to his second wife; two grown children from his first marriage, none from number two. Rita's take on him was the same as mine: shrewd and sly. "I wouldn't want to buy a house from him," she said, and even though she'd laughed, I had the feeling she meant it. He took annual one-week fishing vacations by himself, each year to a different location. But he didn't do much fishing, mostly just sat around and drank beer and schmoozed with whoever happened to be handy. He occupied cabin one, on the south side lakefront. Which meant that his transportation was a four-by-four Chevy Tracker; I could see it parked in front of number one when I came outside.

I went that way long enough to make a mental note of the license plate number, then walked back and across to cabin eight. No sign of the Jeep Cherokee. And no answer to my knock. Each cabin had a tiny porch tacked onto its lake side; I moved around to this one's, climbed three steps onto its weathered boards. A plastic picnic cooler sat in the shade against the wall, but there wasn't anything inside except an inch of melted icewater. The curtains were partially drawn across the window, so I put my nose up to the glass and peered inside. That didn't buy me anything, either. The interior was messy, the bed unmade and clothes and fishing equipment strewn around. Dyce was a slob; so what? There was nothing out of the ordinary that I could see.

I kept my hand off the handle on the porch door. Too early in the game for illegal trespass without provocation, even if the door happened to be unlocked. Instead, I went down and wandered along the narrow strip of beach that ran behind the cabins.

Hal Cantrell was sitting on the porch of cabin one, feet propped on the railing, a bottle of Beck's sweating in one hand. He waved the bottle as I approached and called out, "Hey there. Come on up and join me."

I did that. Next to his chair was a table that held a bucket of ice and more beer, and a pair of six- or seven-power binoculars with a worn leather strap.

"How about a cold one?" he asked.

"Little early for me."

"Me, too, if I weren't on vacation. Might

as well live it up. You never know, right?"

"About what?"

"How long you're going to be around. One day you're above ground, the next you could be under it."

"Like Nils Ostergaard."

"Like him. Hell of a thing, wasn't it."

"Hell of a thing," I agreed.

"Nosy old bird, but I liked him."

"So did I."

Cantrell tilted his head back to get a better look at me from under the brim of his canvas fisherman's hat. "You really think it was an accident?"

"Why? Don't you?"

"Everybody seems to read it that way. But you were asking a mess of questions before the deputies showed up."

"Just my nature. I'm a professional skeptic."

"So am I, when it comes to John Q. Public. Can't survive in my business if you're not."

"Mine, either."

"That fellow Strayhorn," he said. "What's his problem?"

"Problem?"

"The way he kept needling you. Plain he's got a bone on where you're concerned. How come?"

"He doesn't approve of my fishing methods."

"No, huh?"

I shrugged. "You know anything about him?"

"Not much. Makes pipe down in the Central Valley." Cantrell grinned, winked. "Me, now, I'd rather lay pipe on the coast."

"What kind does he make?"

"Sewer pipe, I think he said."

"Have his own company?"

"Could be. Didn't tell me if he does."

"You spend much time with him?"

"Nope. He's not the social type."

"Neither is Fred Dyce."

"Hell, no. *He's* got a bone on for everybody."

"Give you any trouble?"

"Not me. I steer clear of guys like him when they're boozing."

"Any idea what put that chip on his shoulder?"

"Nope, and I could care less."

"Not much of a fisherman," I said, "even though he pretends to be. Doesn't seem to know a dry fly from a housefly."

"You can say that again."

"What do you suppose he's doing here, then?"

"Trying to learn how to be what he says

he is." Cantrell gave me another head-tilted look. "You seem pretty interested in Dyce."

"I'm interested in everybody. Another part of my nature."

"You go around looking in everybody's windows, like you were doing over at Dyce's cabin?"

I didn't answer the question, watching him. His expression didn't change; his eyes remained friendly, guileless. Pretty soon I said, "Nice pair of binoculars you've got there."

"Had 'em twenty years. Can't beat Zeiss."

"For what? Spying?"

He grinned, put his hand over his heart the way he had at the gas pumps yesterday. "I am not a spy. Or a Peeping Tom. Just a guy with a nosy streak, like you and Ostergaard."

"Uh-huh."

"I happened to be scanning around, and I swung the glasses over that way and there you were, up on the porch. So I kept watching. What were you looking for in Dyce's cabin?"

"Nothing in particular. Just looking."

"Wouldn't be because you think Dyce had something to do with the old man's death?"

"No. We all decided it was an accident, remember?"

"Oh sure, I remember."

"I understand Ostergaard had a little run-in with Dyce just after he arrived."

"Is that right? About what?"

"Him pretending to be an expert fisherman. Nils didn't like people who weren't what they claimed to be."

"Who does?"

"You get to know him at all?"

"Who? Ostergaard?"

"Ostergaard."

Another grin. "Now we're around to me. I'm on the list, too, huh?"

"What list is that?"

"The suspect list."

"There is no suspect list," I said. "I wasn't implying anything, Cantrell. About you or anybody else."

"Just asking questions to pass the time of day."

"More or less."

"Okay, here's my answer. No, I didn't know the old man except to say hello to. Didn't exchange more than fifty words with him, most of those the day I got here. He was active and I'm lazy as hell — no common ground." The grin had become a smirk by this time. "Sure you won't have a beer?"

"I'm sure." I pushed away from the railing. "I'd better be moving along."

"Come back any time."

"Maybe I'll do that."

"Meantime, good luck with your fishing," he said as I stepped down off the porch, and when I glanced back at him, he winked again. Broadly. To let me know he hadn't meant the sport.

Nobody was home at the cottage Jacob Strayhorn had rented, a bungalow-style A-frame crowded by dogwood bushes on its west side and fronted by a stubby platform porch. Out in a boat somewhere, I thought. Nosed in between the bushes and the porch was his ten-year-old Chrysler, its low-slung tan body disfigured by dings, dents, and paint scrapes. I noted the license plate number before I drove on.

At the Zaleski cabin I keyed open the door, took half a dozen steps along the hallway — and froze in place with the skin bunching and rippling along the saddle of my back. It was not anything I saw or heard, it was something in the air: emanations, vibes, whatever you want to call it. You get feelings like that when you've been a cop of one kind or another as long as I have and you learn to accept them without question.

Somebody'd been in the cabin since Chuck and I had left this morning. Not the boy and not his mother — somebody who didn't belong.

Still here? It didn't feel that way, but I went straight to the fireplace and caught up a chunk of firewood. The irony in that stayed with me, a bitter taste, as I made a quick search through the rooms.

Long gone. And nothing disturbed or missing that I could spot on a second, more careful check. My fly case was where I'd left it, my underwear and socks and shirts were as I'd arranged them in the dresser. I'd neglected to lock the closet door, but when I looked inside I found that the gun cabinet was still secure, the rifle and shotgun untouched.

Well? A daylight B & E just for a look around?

Except that it hadn't quite been a B & E. There were no signs of forcible entry on the front door lock, on any of the window latches or on the sliding-glass door to the deck. Had I forgotten to lock something besides the closet and he'd just walked in and then secured the place before leaving? Not much sense in that. Let himself in with a key? That was more likely; Nils Ostergaard may have had one and it could've been lifted

164

off him sometime after he was dead. But that still didn't explain the intruder's motivation.

I slid the deck door open all the way, opened a couple of the windows for cross-ventilation, and switched on the ceiling fan — mostly to get rid of trapped heat, partly to banish the bad air the intruder had left behind. Then I washed up, made a sandwich I didn't much want, popped a beer I did want, and put in a collect call to Tamara at my office.

"Yo, chief," she said. "Checking up on me, huh?"

"No way."

"How's Deep Mountain Lake?"

"Peaceful," I said, which was not quite a lie.

"How many trout you murdered so far?"

"Only one. The reason I called —"

"Not much happening here," she said. "I finished the Dalway skip-trace, no problem. Oh, yeah, Bill Gates called, wanted us to handle security for Microsoft at three mil per year. I told him we were too busy and besides, you think computers're tools of the debbil."

"Soul-stealers, right, so you better watch out. Listen, I need you to do something for me."

"Sure, what?"

"Background checks on three men. ASAP."

"Hey, what's this? You *working* up there?"

"No. Doing a favor for a friend."

"Uh-huh. Heard that one before."

"Tamara —"

"How extensive? The checks, I mean."

"Depends. What I'm looking for is anything out of the ordinary, anything crooked or shady or even antisocial. Criminal records or ties. Mental problems. Like that."

"How come? Who are these three guys?"

"Two of them are probably average citizens. The third one . . . well, he may be mixed up in a felony."

"And you don't know which of 'em it is."

"That's it."

"Why not let the local fuzz handle it?"

"It's not an official case. Not yet."

"Okay. Names, addresses?"

"No street addresses; all I've got are cities." I gave her the information I'd gathered on Dyce, Strayhorn, and Cantrell.

"Not much to work with," she said.

"It ought to be enough. Anything you find out, call me right away," and I added the phone number.

"I'm on it right now. You want me to keep working after five? Double-time if I do, remember."

"You won't let me forget. You mind?"

"Money's one thing I never mind." She paused and then said, "Tell you something."

"What's that?"

"Man, you work too hard, you know what I'm saying? One of these days you really ought to take a vacation."

10

Dull, static afternoon. I sweated my way through a restless nap, debated going for a swim, decided the icy water would probably do more harm than good, and settled for a shower instead. Then I packed up my fishing gear, locked it away in the trunk of the car. Funny, but I had no second thoughts, no sense of nostalgia: I simply was not a fisherman any longer. It was as if the sport had given me up, rather than the other way around. I remembered a woman saying to me once that she hadn't quit smoking, smoking had quit her; she'd awakened one morning and reached for her cigarettes, as was her habit, and suddenly the thought of lighting one made her physically ill. She'd never lit up again, she told me. I hadn't quite believed her, but I believed her now, fifteen years later. It can happen that way, all right. Vices, hobbies, other pursuits. Relationships, too. One day there's interest, desire, some degree of passionate involvement, the next it's gone with no real sense of decline or transition, as if it had never existed in the first place.

I wondered briefly if it could happen that

way with Kerry and me, one or the other of us. But it was not anything that worried me, really. You don't love the way she and I loved and have it end all of a sudden, overnight. There's too much at stake on both sides. The ardor cools a little, the relationship changes and goes through its crises big and small, but there is no abrupt termination. If we ever split up — and I was as sure we wouldn't as I could ever be of anything in this life — we would both see it coming long before it reached critical mass.

Around five I went over to the Dixons'. No answer to my knock, so I took myself down to the dock. It and the deck above were deserted, but I heard sounds from the storeroom and saw that its door stood open. As I started up there, Chuck emerged carrying his father's heavy tackle box and an armload of fishing poles and a wicker creel.

"Oh, hi," he said when he saw me. Not much enthusiasm; there was a listlessness in the way he looked and moved.

"Hi. What're you up to?"

"Not much. Just moving Dad's stuff inside, so it'll be ready when he gets here."

"He call since your mom talked to him?"

"No. Jeez, I hope he comes up tomorrow."

"He will if he can possibly get away."

"Yeah, I know."

"That tackle box looks pretty heavy. How about letting me lug it inside?"

He hesitated, then let me take it. "Dad's got a lot more junk in there than I remember."

"Lead sinkers, feels like."

"Some of those, yeah, no kidding. He's had junk like that since he was my age and he won't get rid of it."

"Sentimental, your old man."

"I guess."

We went up into the house and set Pat Dixon's gear in a corner of the living room. "Where's your mom?" I asked. "Still at the Ostergaards'?"

"Yeah. She called a few minutes ago, she'll be back pretty soon. She said you went over there to see Mrs. Ostergaard before she did."

"Just for a few minutes."

"How come? You hardly knew Mr. Ostergaard."

"I knew him well enough to like him and want to pay my respects to his widow."

"I oughta go see her, too," Chuck said. "But I can't make myself do it, not yet, anyway." His mouth tightened; the moistness that came into his eyes made him turn away from me. "Shit. Why'd a thing like that have to happen? Mr. Ostergaard, he was . . . I dunno, he was like my grandfather or something."

"Bad things happen to good people, Chuck."

"I know. Never to the bad ones, the assholes."

"Them, too. Sooner or later."

"Somebody like Mr. Ostergaard . . . you think he's gonna live forever, you know? I mean, he was old but he seemed kind of . . ."

"Indestructible?"

"Yeah. He was always here, every summer, and you think he's always gonna be here, that things'll never change."

"Nothing stays the same, Chuck."

"Sure, but when something crazy happens . . ."

"You deal with it, hard as it is."

"Life's hard and then you die," he said. "I saw that on a T-shirt once. I thought it was funny."

"But you don't think so now."

"No. Not anymore."

"That's good."

"Why's it good?"

"You're growing up," I said. "Kids look at things one way, adults another. The way you feel now is the way a man feels, a man who has compassion for others."

He was making eye contact again. He

said, "I guess you know all about stuff like this. I mean, you've lived a long time, too, seen a lot . . ."

"More than my share."

"Does it still bother you? When people die, people you want to keep on living?"

"Always has, always will."

"So how do *you* deal with it?"

"By trying to keep it in perspective. There's nothing wrong with hurting or feeling sad or angry or confused, as long as you don't let those feelings control you. Life goes on, you have to go on, too. Focus on the good parts, on being good yourself, and you can get through anything bad that comes along."

He took a few seconds to digest that. Then, "You know something? You're a lot like my dad. He says stuff like that, not the same but stuff that makes me feel better because I know it has to be true."

"Your dad's a good man."

"You're pretty cool, too," he said shyly. There was an awkward moment, as there must be between father and son when they have this kind of talk. A grin, then, and some of the natural animation was back in his voice when he said, "Hey, you want a beer? We've got some cold in the fridge."

"Sure. I can use one."

"I'll get it."

He hurried off into the kitchen, and I decided I'd handled the situation about as well as I could. I hadn't said anything profound, but the sense of the words were what he'd needed to hear. The male bond, as Marian had called it. I was glad the session was over, but it hadn't been as difficult as I'd expected and it had left me feeling better, too — and a little ashamed at the bitterness I'd felt earlier. I wondered if I'd have made a good father and thought, yeah, I probably would have. It was a comforting thought, one mixed with a certain amount of regret.

Chuck came back with a long-necked Bud, watched me take a pull on it before he said, "How about tomorrow? You want to go fishing at Chuck's Hole again?"

I hated to disappoint him, but there was only one answer I could give. When you're through with an activity, you're through with it; I would not put myself through any more pretense even for him. "I can't, Chuck. I've got some business to take care of in the morning."

"Can't it wait until after noon?"

"I'm afraid not."

He took it in stride. "Hey, that's okay, I understand. Maybe —"

He broke off at the rising whine of a boat's engine, windblown through the open doors to the deck. I followed him over there, saw a dark green rowboat with an attached kicker angling in toward the Dixons' dock. The man bent forward from the tiller was Jacob Strayhorn.

Chuck said, "Wonder why he came back?"

"Back?"

"He was here a while ago, before you came over."

"What'd he want?"

"Nothing much. Just to talk."

"About Nils?"

"Mostly, yeah."

Strayhorn bumped the rowboat's prow against the float, shut off the panting kicker. Chuck got down there in time to wind the painter around one of the cleats. The expression on Strayhorn's face, I saw as he climbed out, was oddly intense. His features seemed harder, less bland, under a thin film of sweat.

"Saw you two carrying fishing gear," he said. "Planning to go out before dark?"

"Nah," Chuck said, "we were just moving my dad's stuff inside the house."

"Just moving it, that's all?"

"Yeah."

"Not because he'll be here tomorrow?"

"Well, he still hasn't let us know, but I sure hope he will."

I said, "You an evening fisherman, Strayhorn?"

"I can take it or leave it. Why?"

"Just wondering why you should care whether Chuck and I were going out before dark."

"I don't, particularly. Thought I'd go along if you were."

"I like fishing at dusk myself. Rivers more than lakes. You ever go after bass in the San Joaquin sloughs?"

"Where? Oh, the San Joaquin River. Once or twice."

"Venice Island? Potato Slough?"

"That general area."

"How about the Delta?"

"How about it?"

"Favorite spot in there?"

"One's as good as another."

"I'm partial to Dead Man's Slough. You know it?"

"No."

"Sycamore Slough? Hog Slough?"

"No."

"Where do you go for crayfish? Channel cats?"

"Crayfish?"

"Delta's full of 'em. Or didn't you know that?"

His eyes, pale and squinty, flicked over my face. It was like being strafed by bugs. There was none of the low-key smarminess about him today; he seemed both hyped and irritated. It was plain that he didn't care for the kind of questions I was asking. That made us even: I didn't care for his answers.

I said, "I guess you don't do much fishing close to home."

"That's right," he said flatly, "I don't. I prefer the mountains. Trout streams."

"Uh-huh."

"And I know what to do with one when I catch it." He turned his attention to Chuck. "Maybe you and me'll go out one of these mornings. What do you say?"

"Well . . ." The boy glanced at me and then said to Strayhorn, "Tomorrow's about the only day. Unless my dad doesn't drive up until Wednesday."

"Tomorrow's good for me. What time?"

"Earlier the better. Five-thirty?"

"Five-thirty it is."

"I know a good spot. Don't I, Bill?"

"One of the best," I said.

"Chuck's Hole. I named it after myself because I'm the one who found it."

"Good for you," Strayhorn said. "Meet you here?"

"Sure. We'll take our skiff."

Strayhorn nodded, and without acknowledging me again he swung back into the rowboat. I watched him shove away from the dock, fire up the kicker, and go skimming off toward his rented cottage.

Chuck said, a little defensively, "It's no fun fishing alone. And Mom won't get up early enough. But I'd rather go with you."

"Thanks."

"You can still come along. I wish you would."

"I don't know, maybe." Distracted response; I was thinking about Strayhorn.

My misgivings about the man were stronger now than ever. For somebody who claimed to be a Stockton native, he didn't know a damned thing about either the San Joaquin River or the Sacramento Delta, both of which were practically in Stockton's backyard.

It was nearly six-thirty when I walked into Judson's cafe. Two of the tables were occupied with beer drinkers carrying on the wake for Nils Ostergaard, but only one of the stools at the bar had a pair of hams perched on it — Fred Dyce's. I wondered why he

177

was hunched there alone until I sat down next to him and got a good look at his face. It had a dark, broody cast, like the sky before a thunderstorm. And the slackness of his mouth, the glaze on his eyes, the empty beer bottle and empty shot glass in front of him told the rest of the story. Wherever he'd been all afternoon, it was a place that had plenty of liquor. He was about as deep in the bag as you can get and still remain upright.

"Hello, Dyce."

His head turned slowly and he squinted at me as if I were a bug that had landed too close to him. "Go 'way," he said.

"Now, that's no way to be."

"Go 'way."

"What're you celebrating?"

"Celebrating. Shit."

"Little early in the evening for such a big heat."

The squinty eyes showed aggression. "None a your goddamn business what I do."

"Probably not. Unless you want to talk about it."

"Talk about what?"

"Whatever's eating at you."

"Nothing eating at me." Automatic response; the next words out of his mouth made it a lie. "You had my prollems you'd get shit-faced too."

"What problems?"

"None a your goddamn business. Buy me a drink or go 'way."

Rita had been hovering nearby. When she heard that last she moved closer; the look she gave me said that she wanted him out of there and she'd be grateful for any help. Mack must be off someplace; if he were around, Dyce would already be gone.

She said, "I think you've had enough, Mr. Dyce."

"Hell I have," he said.

"Mrs. Judson's right," I said. "How about some coffee?"

"Jack Daniel's, double shot. Beer chaser."

"Coffee," I said to Rita. "Same for me."

She mouthed the word "Thanks" and moved off. Dyce muttered something I didn't catch. He peered at me again, blearily, and said, "You married man?"

"Yep."

"Marriage sucks. Don't ever get married."

"Why is that?"

"Work your ass off for 'em, give 'em everything they want, and what happens? They screw you, that's what happens. Screwin' you get ain't worth screwin' you got."

"Your wife's divorcing you, is that it?"

"Sixteen years," Dyce said. "Sixteen years, come home one night, she says it ain't workin' no more, Freddy, I want out." His voice rose. "Sixteen fuckin' years!"

"Easy, Fred. This is a public place."

"Fuck her and fuck you, too," he said, but not as loud. "Go 'way, lemme drink in peace."

Rita came back with two cups of coffee, set one in front of each of us. Dyce stared into the steam rising from his. "What's this?"

"Coffee. Better drink it."

"Don't want any goddamn coffee. Jack Daniel's, double shot. Beer chaser."

"You've had enough alcohol."

"Who're you, tell me I had enough?"

"Just a guy trying to be your friend."

"Friend, hell. I got no friends. Just Connie and she don't want me no more." Another squint. The eyes had moisture in them now. Crying jag coming on, I thought. "Called her up 'safternoon, ask her gimme 'nother chance, you know what it got me? Huh?"

"What'd it get you?"

"Kick inna gut, that's what. Some guy answered, some goddamn *guy*. Her phone, my phone, she's screwin' some sonabitch in *my* house. What you think a that, huh?"

"What did the guy say?"

"Say? Who cares what the sonabitch said. Listen, I doan wanna talk about it no more."

"Okay with me. Drink your coffee and we'll get out of here."

"Get out? Why?"

"We'll go to your cabin."

"Hell we will. What're you, a fag?"

"You got any liquor in your cabin?"

"Huh?"

"Liquor. In your cabin."

"Sure I got some. What the hell?"

"How about we go there and have a drink together?"

"Doan wanna drink with you. Tell you what I wanna do. Go home, kick Connie's ass, 'at's what. Kick sonabitch's ass, too. Kick both their asses, screwin' him in *my* house."

"Tomorrow, Fred. You can go home to-morrow."

"Quit tellin' me what to do!"

I'd misread him. Either that or his drunken temperament was so mercurial he was totally unpredictable. He shoved away from the bar, almost toppling his stool and himself, managed to stay upright, and stood swaying and glaring at me.

"Oughta kick *your* fag ass," he said.

The half-dozen people left in there were staring at us. But nobody was moving; whatever happened was up to me. I sighed, thinking: I don't need this now, I've had enough for one day. I eased off my stool so as not to provoke him with any sudden movements.

"Okay, Fred," I said. "Let's go outside."

"What?"

"Outside. You can kick my ass outside."

"Wrong with right here, huh?"

I crowded him a little. "Outside, buddy."

"Screw you."

"Outside."

He made a throat noise and swung at me.

It was more pathetic than anything else. Telegraphed punch, and no steam in it, like a movie attack in slow motion. I caught his arm, twisted it and his body, hammerlocked the arm against his backbone, and marched him grunting and swearing to the door, outside, and straight across to his cabin. There was nothing he could do about it, his feet slipping and sliding every time he tried to put up a struggle. When we got to the cabin, I shoved him up flat against the door and held him there while I tried the knob. It wasn't locked. I got it open, shoved him through and into the bedroom and threw him facedown across the bed, still hanging on to his arm.

"You're home, Freddy boy," I said, "and when I let you go, you'd better stay right here. You hear me? Stay put or I'll really hurt you."

I released him, backed off a couple of steps. He lay there for maybe fifteen seconds, then rolled over and managed to sit up. All the aggression was gone from his face; it had become saggy with drunken bewilderment. He peered up at me, massaging his arm.

"Whassa idea?" he said. "Almost bust my goddamn arm."

In the next second, with no warning at all, he started to bawl like a baby.

I'm on Connie's side, I thought disgustedly. Whoever her new boyfriend is, he's got to be an improvement.

I left the cabin and returned to the main building. Some of the people who'd witnessed the little episode were standing out front; none of them had anything to say as I approached Rita, who was filling the doorway to the cafe.

She thanked me, and I said, "Sure. Sorry I couldn't get him out sooner, without the hassle. But he's too far gone to listen to reason."

"I shouldn't've served him when he came in, not even one round."

"Well, I doubt he'll be any more trouble tonight. But if he does come back, give me a call."

"Not necessary. Mack'll be home from Quincy pretty soon. How about something on the house, a drink or some food?"

"I've lost my thirst and my appetite. But thanks anyway."

So much for Dyce, I thought as I got into the car. He's not the one. Poor self-pitying slob with a mad-on against the world because his wife is divorcing him for another man; a scratch fighter and a blowhard and a fool, but nothing more.

If Ostergaard *was* murdered by a first-timer, it was either Strayhorn or Cantrell.

11

As soon as I entered the Zaleski cabin, I had the same sudden, violated-space feeling I'd experienced earlier. Not a leftover current but a fresh one. My skin prickled with it; the hair on my scalp rippled.

Without touching the light switch, I backed out and shut the door. It took me thirty seconds to unlock the car, remove the .38 Colt Bodyguard from its clips under the dash, get back to the door and inside. I stood listening. No sounds, nothing for my eyes to pick up except stationary shadows. I clicked on the hall light, went from there into the empty kitchen. Put on the kitchen light and followed its outspill into the front room. Empty. Same with both bedrooms and the bathroom between them. And again, nothing seemed to have been disturbed.

I let myself relax, lowering the gun. Definitely a fresh aura, though; there hadn't been anything left of the first one after I'd aired the place out this afternoon. Somebody had been here again tonight — the same somebody. Twice in one day.

For what damn purpose?

I started back to the front door, to see if there were any signs of forced entry this time — and there was a knock outside. I froze. A second knock sounded; that one took me over beside the door, with the gun up alongside my ear.

"Yes?"

"It's Marian."

She sounded all right, nothing unnatural or urgent in her voice. I slipped the .38 into my jacket pocket, but I kept my hand on it as I opened the door.

She was alone. A quick study, too; she said immediately, "You're all tense. Is something wrong?"

"No. Just feeling jumpy tonight, I guess." My face had a damp feel; I let go of the gun, used both hands to dry my cheeks and forehead. "What can I do for you, Marian?"

"Well, I have a message for you."

"Message?"

"From Callie Ostergaard. Something she forgot to tell you, she said. About Nils — a receipt he found the other day that bothered him."

"What kind of receipt?"

"Callie doesn't know. That was all he told her."

"Does she know where he found it?"

"No."

"In what way was he bothered by it?"

"Puzzled and suspicious, Callie said." Light from the hall showed vertical ridges between Marian's eyes, like close-set quote marks. "What's this about? Why should Callie want me to tell you about a receipt?"

"I can't talk about it now. It's between Callie and me."

"Something to do with what happened to Nils?"

"Marian, please don't ask me. I'll explain it to you when I can. Okay?

"This receipt. Does Callie know what Nils did with it?"

"Not exactly."

"Meaning she has an idea where it might be?"

"Yes. She said for you to look in the toolbox in Nils's pickup. He kept things in there that he didn't want to bring into the house for one reason or another — private things. She doesn't know where the pickup is now."

"Where he left it last night," I said, "or else it's been moved over to Judson's." Then, because I'd never seen him driving it, "What make and color?"

"A Ford, I think. At least fifteen years old. White with one of those covered shells on the back."

"Will I need a key to get into the toolbox?"

"Callie didn't say anything about a key."

"Probably not, then. While we're on the subject of keys . . . did Nils have one to your cabin?"

"Yes, he did."

"To this one, too?"

She nodded. "He had spare keys to several of the cottages in case of emergency."

"Where'd he keep them? At home, on his person?"

"He carried them on a big ring."

"Each one marked?"

"Yes, a piece of tape with the owner's name."

"Thanks, Marian. Forgive me for being mysterious. It's just that I don't want to say anything until I have more information."

She said, "I understand," and let it go. Most people wouldn't have; she was a special person, all right. "Good night."

"Good night."

I watched her out of sight, thinking: So somebody could've taken the Zaleski key off Nils's body and used it to get in here both times. Taken it after he was murdered, if he was murdered, or this morning after the body was found. His entire key ring could've been lifted, for that matter.

Why? Why would anybody go to the trouble to steal Ostergaard's keys and then risk not one but two covert visits to this cabin?

Why would anybody steal padlocks off boathouse and storeroom doors?

Why would anybody pretend to be someone he isn't at a remote mountain lake? And then maybe commit murder to protect his real identity?

Erratic, apparently purposeless behavior. The stuff of paranoia and psychosis . . .

I got into the car again, not bothering to lock the cabin, and drove down to Judson's. The pickup Marian had described had been moved there; it was parked at the western edge of the lot. I pulled in close next to it. There was activity inside the cafe but nobody outside in the vicinity. I went to the Ford, tried the lift-up door on the shell. It wasn't locked. The sky was darkening, with most of the sun gone behind the peaks to the west, but there was still enough daylight for me to see inside and to find the toolbox among a welter of fishing gear, spare parts, and miscellany. I flipped its catches, sifted through the contents.

At the bottom, tucked inside a plastic freezer bag, were a few personal papers and a small envelope. The envelope yielded a strip of paper about four inches long, rumpled and food stained and folded in half — a cash register receipt. I shoved it into my pocket, closed the toolbox and the shell door, and drove straight back to the cabin.

In the privacy of the kitchen I examined the cash register receipt. It was from a Safeway store and carried a list of fourteen items ranging from Hormel chili with beans to Elmer's Glue to a six-pack of Beck's. Dated twelve days ago. None of that was particularly interesting; the only thing about the receipt that pushed any buttons was the location of the Safeway branch.

Half Moon Bay.

Why would Ostergaard keep a Safeway receipt that, judging from the food stains, he'd found in somebody's garbage? Why would he poke around in garbage in the first place? And why would the receipt puzzle him, make him suspicious?

Hal Cantrell, I thought. He lived and worked in Pacifica, which was only about fifteen miles up the coast from Half Moon Bay. And he'd been drinking a bottle of Beck's this afternoon. Coincidence or connection? Maybe —

The telephone went off.

The sudden noise made me jump. Getting nervy. Hell, who wouldn't under the circumstances? I went over and answered the thing.

Tamara. She said, "Yo, finally," with a slight prickly edge in her voice. "This the fourth time I done called you, boss man. I even tried your car phone."

"I've been in and out and I didn't expect you to get back to me tonight. Something already?"

"Yep. Fast worker you got here. Fast and underpaid, you know what I'm saying?"

I ignored that. "Talk to me. What've you got?"

"Nothing on Fred Dyce or Hal Cantrell. Mr. John Strayhorn, now, he's something else. Gotta be your man."

"Strayhorn? Why?"

"Looking for a man's not who he says he is, right?"

"And Strayhorn's not?"

"Well, he doesn't live in Stockton or anywhere else down that way. And there isn't any company that manufactures sewer pipe in the Valley, either. No Jacob Strayhorn anywhere in Norcal, only three J. Strayhorns and none of 'em owns a Chrysler LeBaron. Two of the three were home, not off on a fishing trip in the mountains. I couldn't get hold of the third, but since her first name's Jolene I don't think she's your man."

"Criminal record on anyone named Strayhorn?"

"Nope. Not in California and not with the feds, either. Phony name, probably."

"Why pick a name like Jacob Strayhorn for an alias?"

"Hey, you can answer that better'n me."

"I don't have any answers right now," I said. "Were you able to trace the license plate number I gave you?"

"Yup. Belongs to a ten-year-old Chrysler LeBaron, all right, but the registered owner's name is Ed Farlow."

"Located where?"

"South San Francisco. But he's not Strayhorn."

"You talked to him?"

"Yup. He sold the car about six weeks ago, through an ad in the *Chronicle*. Guess the name of the dude that bought it."

"Jacob Strayhorn."

"You got it. Paid eight hundred cash."

"And never bothered to reregister. Did you ask Farlow to describe the buyer?"

"Said he couldn't remember much about the man. Said he was white, middle-aged, average —"

"— and had pale eyes."

"Right. Fits your man, huh?"

"To a T. I don't supposed he volunteered any information to Farlow?"

"Nope, and Mr. F. didn't ask."

"How'd he get to Farlow's home? Somebody drive him?"

"Mr. F. doesn't know. Had a call asking if the car was still for sale, couple of hours later Strayhorn showed up on his doorstep. That's all he remembers."

I sat down and muttered, "What the hell."

"Say what?"

"Talking to myself."

"So what's this dude up to? What's happening up there?"

"Tamara, I don't have any damn idea."

"But you're gonna find out, am I right?"

"If I can."

"Anything more you want me to do?"

"Not tonight. I'll let you know."

"Well, stay cool. Hang loose."

"Hang and rattle, more likely."

"Huh?"

"Old expression. Don't worry about me."

"Who says I'm worried?"

"I can hear it in your voice."

"Maybe I am," she said. "You still owe me ten days' pay," and there was a gentle click as she broke the connection.

I opened a bottle of Bud, then decided I

didn't want it after all and forced the cap back on and put the bottle away in the fridge. I wandered into the front room, then out onto the deck. Dark now. Running clouds obscured some of the stars, giving the lake a black, oily sheen. I stared down at the water, trying to make at least some of what I knew add up.

Fat chance. I was more confused now than before Tamara's call.

Strayhorn wasn't Strayhorn, evidently, but I still had no clue as to who or what he really was. Maybe he'd murdered Nils Ostergaard and maybe he hadn't. Maybe he was the one who'd trespassed here twice today and maybe he wasn't. Maybe there was a link between him and Half Moon Bay that explained why Ostergaard had kept the Safeway receipt — and maybe there wasn't. The whole business was a maze of half-formed possibilities and deadends. And I was like the laboratory rat running around banging into walls and corners, looking for a way through to the cheese.

From the Notebooks of
Donald Michael Latimer

Mon., July 1 — 11:00 P.M.

Bomb signature. Bomb signature!

What's the matter with me? I know how advanced forensics have become, I should've foreseen the danger, yet it never even occurred to me until the kid bragged about it this afternoon. Careless. Stupid. Each of the devices for Cotter and the judge was different, I made sure of that, but I used pretty much the same types of materials for both — same types I used five years ago for Kathryn and Lover Boy. Cops haven't got a computer match yet, nothing on the radio and there would be if they had an ID, but they could come up with one any time and if they do they'll know right away that Dixon's my next target, and that I'll be going after Kathryn, too.

I shouldn't have been so wedded to the Plan. That's where I made my mistake, and damn lucky it wasn't a fatal one. Have to change it now, no choice. Can't wait any longer, it's past time for the mountain to go to Mohammed. Do Dixon, then get to Kathryn before she's warned and goes into hiding somewhere.

Wish I could take Dixon's Subdivision (c) boobytrap along with me, it really is perfect, but I'd be a fool to transport it armed the way it is and I don't have time to disassemble and rewire it. I wouldn't even risk bringing it over here now that it's been moved. Too much chance of it blowing up in my face. Have to whip up a new bomb, destructive device, boobytrap for Mr. Prosecutor and I know just what kind, just how to fix him. New plan, and it's a good one. Not quite as fitting but the end result is what matters. And this way the son of a bitch hurts *before* he dies, too, hurts bad. Might turn out to be even better this way, even sweeter. Fix him good and proper.

Fix that bastard private cop, too. He's sniffing close, but I'll be long gone before he gets close enough to do anything except die. Surprise package for him, surprise package for Dixon, then a fast trip to Indiana to give Kathryn her big send-off.

Boom!

BOOM!

B
O
O
M
!

12

Long, restless night. I woke up half a dozen times, the last one at six-twenty. Tuesday A.M. was cloudy, windy, the lake choppy and the color of slate; it matched my mood.

As I stood under the shower I tried again to figure a reasonable plan of action. None of my options looked any better in the daylight than they had during the night. I did not have enough facts to sic the local law on Jacob Strayhorn, whoever the hell he really was; if I even hinted that he might be guilty of a homicide, and it turned out he was an innocent party and had more or less legitimate reasons for using an alias, I was wide open for all sorts of legal ramifications. So the thing to do was to gather more information. Which meant another talk with him, and if I could work it, a look around his rented cottage when he wasn't there. I didn't much care for that last, but if it became necessary I'd have to risk it. Quid pro quo.

I toweled off, put on a clean shirt, decided a clean pair of trousers was in order as well, and opened the closet door — something I had stupidly neglected to do last night. And then stood flat-footed with my chest going tight.

The Mossberg .410 shotgun was missing.

The gun cabinet's lock had been forced; the glass door wobbled open when I tugged on it. A box of Magnum shells lay on a shelf at the bottom. Just one box — and I was pretty sure there'd been two.

Now I knew part of the reason he'd come here twice yesterday. The first time to look around, and he'd spotted the weapons when he opened the closet door. The second time had been to swipe the Mossberg.

Why? And why hadn't he taken the shotgun on the first pass through?

Strayhorn, dammit, I thought. Has to be.

I was mad as hell by the time I finished dressing. And not all the anger was directed outwardly. I was thinking now, much later than I should've considered it, that Chuck had gone off fishing with Strayhorn this morning. I should have put a stop to that idea last night, after Tamara's call. No reason to believe then or now that Strayhorn had any harmful intentions toward the boy, but that missing shotgun added menace to an already tense situation.

The Colt Bodyguard was on the night-stand where I'd laid it as a nighttime precaution. I zipped it into the pocket of my windbreaker. Next to an assault rifle, a shotgun is the deadliest of small arms, but only at close to medium range; in very tight quarters your self-defense survival rate is a hell of a lot higher with a handgun. The thing to do first of all —

— was to answer the phone. The bell shrilled, slicing through the early-morning quiet, as I came out of the bedroom.

I got it on the second ring, with my eyes on my watch. Seven-ten. A call this early, here, couldn't be anything good.

It wasn't. Pat Dixon's voice said my name interrogatively, then his name without waiting for a reply. There was a quality in it, a kind of suppressed urgency, that screwed the tension in me down another couple of notches.

"Listen," he said, "I need you to do something for me."

"Name it."

"Go get Marian and Chuck and drive them back to the city. Right away."

"What —"

"Don't bring them here — our house. I'll give you another address, friends of ours."

"Okay, but tell me why first."

"Precaution. I don't think . . . I don't want to think they're in any danger up there, but we can't afford to take chances."

"Pat, what's got you so spooked?"

He drew a heavy breath; I heard it hiss like steam when he released it. "We've got a probable ID on the bomber finally. Ninety-five percent probability match. Dave Maccerone just called from the Hall. It looks . . . chances are there's at least a third person and probably more on his hit list. Third one is me."

" . . . Are you sure?"

"Yeah. His name is Latimer, Donald Michael Latimer. Former financial consultant here in the city, fairly successful at one time. Ex-Marine with explosives training. Went over the edge five years ago when he found out his wife was having an affair and put a boobytrap bomb in the trunk of the boy-friend's car, hooked up to the trunk release. It didn't go off because of a bad solder joint, but a second bomb under the back porch of the man's house did go off — cut him up with flying glass and debris. Latimer claimed he didn't intend bodily harm, the bombs were just messages to leave his wife alone."

"You prosecuted the case, is that it?"

"That's it. Doug Cotter and me — Doug was on the D.A.'s staff then. Judge Turn-bull was on the bench." Dixon blew out another ragged breath. "We went after Latimer pretty hard. Mainly because he had a classic profile — intelligent but egocentric, with sociopathic tendencies and a paramilitary attitude. Collected guns, including a couple of semiautomatic weapons. Even had a subscription to *Soldier of Fortune.* Workaholic, too, totally driven. Add all of that together and you had a ticking bomb in human form, capable of much greater violence than he'd shown toward his wife and her lover. We'd have let his lawyers plead him down if he'd been willing to accept psychiatric help, but Latimer refused and insisted on pleading innocent. We felt putting him away for the maximum was our best option. Tried to get him on attempted homicide, but the jury felt there was reasonable doubt on that issue. They convicted on two other counts — explosion of a destructive device and setting booby-traps. Turnbull gave him five years on each count."

"How long was he in prison?"

"Five years total. Paroled seven weeks ago. Maccerone rousted his parole officer out of bed before he called me. Last contact the PO had with Latimer was three weeks ago. He tried to get in touch with him last week, when a job offer came up, couldn't find him, and violated him right away. No indication of Latimer's whereabouts since. There's an APB out on him now."

My stomach had begun to cramp; I sat at the kitchen table, leaning forward to ease the ache. A measure of fear had mixed with the anger in me. I could see the rest of it coming now, like a storm roiling wild and black on a near horizon.

"Maybe he's left the state, maybe he hasn't," Dixon said. "Maccerone thinks there's a chance of it, that's why I'm still . . . why nothing's happened to me yet. But I don't buy it. Best I can figure is that Latimer set a boobytrap for me somewhere and I've been blind lucky enough so far not to trigger it. Charley Seltzer's bringing his bomb techs out here to the house —"

"What was Latimer's last known address?"

". . . What?"

"Latimer. Where was he living the last time his PO saw him?"

"Daly City. He took an apartment there when he was released. But he only stayed a month. The PO should've checked to make sure the address remained current, but he's got a heavy caseload and he screwed up."

"What does Latimer look like?"

"Why? What're you —"

"Come on, Pat. Describe him."

"Midforties, average height, average weight. Brown hair, light-blue eyes . . ."

"Does the name Strayhorn mean anything to you?"

"What name was that?"

"Strayhorn. Jacob Strayhorn."

"How did — Yes, that's the man Latimer's wife was having the affair with. A pharmacist on West Portal. She's married to Strayhorn now, they live in his home state, Indiana, and they're the other possibles on Latimer's hit list. Why the hell are you asking all these questions? You know something, don't you?"

I told him. Quick and terse, not pulling any punches. The only things I didn't go into were the missing shotgun and the fact that his son was very likely in Latimer's company this minute.

"Jesus!" he said when I was done. "You're telling me Latimer's been up there since last Thursday?"

"Waiting for you to show, evidently. He must've found out somehow about your cabin up here and that you were going on vacation."

"I never made a secret of it. But why would he go after me at the lake instead of — Oh shit, you don't think . . ."

"What?"

"Not just me, Marian and Chuck, too?"

"Easy. There's no reason to believe that."

"You've got to get them out of there!"

"I will. Just stay cool. He hasn't done anything to them in four days, he's not going to. It's you he's after."

"But why at the lake? There has to be a reason."

"Whatever it is," I said, "it's keeping him here. Tied in, maybe, with the reason he used different types of bombs on Cotter and Turnbull. Something different for you, too."

"Different. Bombs, boobytraps . . ."

The way he said that prompted me to ask, "Suggest something to you?"

Span of silence. Then Dixon said, talking to himself as much as to me, "Tripwire, that's how Cotter . . . and in the judge's boobytrap, those sharpened steel rods . . . Christ almighty!"

"Pat?"

"Not rods, stakes — sharpened *stakes!* That's why he's up there waiting for me . . . the sick son of a bitch!"

I said sharply, "Make sense."

"His boobytraps, all three of them, must be tied to the penal code."

"I don't follow."

"The statute we convicted him on — the

boobytrap statute, Chapter Three point Two of the California Penal Code. One of the section subdivisions reads . . . let me think . . . it says 'Boobytraps may include but are not limited to explosive devices attached to tripwires or other triggering mechanisms, sharpened stakes, and lines or wire with hooks attached.' Hooks. You see it?"

I saw it, all right, the way Latimer had twisted the statute to suit his own perverted brand of revenge. My hand was slick on the receiver as I got to my feet. "Fishhooks," I said.

"Has to be. Something to do with fishhooks."

And in my mind, then, I was reliving a few minutes of yesterday. Seeing Chuck emerge from the storeroom under the deck, carrying his father's heavy tackle box. Hearing him say *Dad's got a lot more junk in here than I remember.* Feeling the weight of the box as I lugged it up into the cabin, set it on the floor. Not hard enough to jar it, but I could have, and if I had . . .

"Pat," I said, "how fast can you get a bomb squad up here?"

". . . You have an idea where he put it?"

"I think so. Yeah."

"Where, for God's sake?"

"Your tackle box, the one you keep in the storeroom." That's why the padlock was off the storeroom door, I was thinking. The second one, from the boathouse, was to confuse the issue. "How fast on the bomb squad?"

"Nearest one'd be Sacramento. They'd have to assemble and fly in by helicopter . . . couple of hours, soonest."

"Okay. One thing, Pat. I'm not leaving here with your family until I'm sure Latimer has been neutralized."

"That's not your problem. The county sheriff —"

"It'll take him and deputies a while to get here from Quincy." My problem, all right, and for more reasons than that one. "You'll have to call them, let them know. No time for me to do it, and you've got the authority."

"First thing. Where'll they find Latimer?"

I told Dixon which cottage he'd rented. "He may be there, he may not. I'll try to pinpoint him. Have the sheriff look for me at Judson's."

"You make sure Marian and Chuck are safe before you do anything else."

"I will. Have you talked to Marian?"

"This morning? No."

"Well, I doubt they're together. Chuck's

gone fishing at Chuck's Hole. I'll have to go get him." Dixon said something but I kept talking through it. "You do the explaining to Marian — I'll have her call you from Judson's. Don't tell her anything about Strayhorn being Latimer or about the boobytrap. She doesn't need to know any of that yet."

"All right. *Move,* will you?"

"Moving," I said.

I banged the phone down and went out of there on the run.

13

Marian was the first hurdle, the easy one. I hammered on the cabin door, different hopes colliding against one another in my mind: that the joint fishing trip had been canceled and the boy was home or had gone to Chuck's Hole alone, that there hadn't been anything sly or sinister in Latimer's invitation yesterday, that Marian was here for me to talk to, that she wasn't here because then I could get after Chuck, Latimer, both of them that much sooner. . . .

She was there. She opened up after a few seconds, started to smile when she saw me, turned it upside down when she got a good look at my face. "What is it?" she said, alarmed. "What's the matter?"

Not answering, I eased in past her and kept going into the front room. The tackle box was where I'd set it yesterday, against a side wall. Small, cold relief that it hadn't been moved again and made even more dangerous. Latimer's boobytrap bomb wasn't the main worry right now.

Marian had come up behind me. I turned to face her, tried to keep my voice neutral as

I asked, "Chuck go fishing with Jacob Strayhorn this morning?"

"Yes."

"To Chuck's Hole?"

"As far as I know. What in heaven's name —"

"Listen to me, Marian," I said. "I'm going to ask you to trust me and do what I tell you, without question or argument. I just got off the phone with Pat. This is what he wants, too."

She opened her mouth, shut it again, and nodded once.

"Take my car and drive to Judson's." I had the keys in my hand; I pushed them into hers, closed her fingers around them. "Call Pat from there — he's home. He'll explain what this is all about. Then stay there and wait for me. Okay?"

Another nod. "Chuck?" she said.

"I'm going to Chuck's Hole right now. I'll bring him to Judson's as soon as I can."

Her eyes burned into mine, searching. Five, six, seven beats; neither of us blinked or looked away. Then, wordlessly, she caught up her purse from where it was looped over the back of a chair and headed for the door.

I went to the side wall, avoiding the tackle box, and grabbed one of Pat's sacked fishing poles to use for protective coloration. Marian didn't say anything when I came outside with it, nor did she question me when I told her to lock up. Together we went over the rise and onto the Zaleski property, moving fast but not running. She gave me one last look before we parted, her for the car and me for the dock and Zaleski's skiff; it told me what she was thinking and made me grit my teeth, the sweat run on my upper body.

He's in your hands. Don't let anything happen to him.

I won't, I vowed. My fault if he's harmed in any way and how could I ever forgive myself for that?

I threw the sacked pole into the skiff, clambered in after it. The outboard was cold and cranky; it took three or four minutes and a string of cusswords to get it working. What if it quit on me before I got over there? No, the hell with that kind of thinking. If it quit, I'd fix it; the screwdriver Nils Ostergaard had given me was still wedged under the seat.

Out on the lake, with the throttle wide open, I beat myself up a little more by wondering if I should have made the connection last night between what had been happening up here and the bombing threat against Pat Dixon. The missing padlocks, Ostergaard's suspicions and his sudden death, the news that Strayhorn wasn't Strayhorn . . . was there enough in that to intimate a plot against Dixon, a link with the San Francisco bombings? Maybe not. Probably not. Quantum leap from one to the other without so much as a hint that Dixon was number three on the bomber's hit list. I'm not psychic and I'm not Sherlock Holmes. Still . . . I'd taken long speculative leaps before, made connections that at the time had seemed farfetched. Slipping. Losing the intuitive edge I'd once had. At the least I should've smelled enough wrong to keep the kid away from Strayhorn this morning. . . .

Get off that, too. What's done is done, what's coming is all that matters. No mistakes when you get to Chuck's Hole, when you drop the fisherman's pose and the gun comes out.

The outboard sputtered and rattled a couple of times as I neared the far shore, but it didn't conk out on me. No time lost on that account. Five minutes lost on another, though: I thought I was pointed straight for the inlet that led to Chuck's Hole, but it had been pre-dawn when the boy took me into it, and coming out I had not had a good look at landmarks, so I missed it now by a couple of hundred yards. I had to swing back and forth twice before I spotted the right opening in the dense forest growth.

Sweat soaked my shirt as I eased in there, turned clammy once I was out of the sun and into the dank, murky woods. I cut the engine, hauled up one of the oars and poled upstream the way Chuck had, through a hundred yards of twists and turns. I could hear the snowmelt bubbling down the terraced rise before I saw the series of steps themselves. The mud beach where we'd left the Dixon boat was hidden for another few seconds, then it slid into view —

Empty.

No sign of Chuck's skiff or any other.

Ripples on my back as I poled closer for a better look at the beach. What marks remained there were not fresh; no craft and no people had been here this morning.

The shape of what Latimer was up to began to come clear then — and I damned myself again for not anticipating the possibility. Savagely I slashed at the water with the oar, slashed at the bank and the snarls of tree roots until I got the skiff turned around and moving downstream. The return trip seemed to take twice as long, even though the current helped carry me along. When I came into the sun glare on the lake, I was breathing hard and my head felt swollen, blood-heavy. The outboard fired instantly; I opened the throttle wide, heading south-west.

There were other boats out now. Somebody hailed me from one — Cantrell, I think — but I barely glanced his way. I sat bowed forward, staring at the line of cottages along the south shore. Buildings seldom look the same from lakeside as they do from a shore road, despite the fact that each was different enough from its neighbors. It was not until I'd come to within a hundred yards of the shoreline, running parallel to it, that I was able to pick out the green-shingled A-frame with the dogwood bushes along its west side.

A skiff was tied to the dock float, a piece of canvas thrown over it. The canvas failed to cover it completely; I could tell from forty yards off that it wasn't the rented craft Strayhorn — Latimer — had been piloting last night. It was the Dixon boat. No question of that, either.

I came in too fast, banged the prow and the port side against the float end before I got the power shut all the way down. The skiff bounced off, nearly capsized. I had to come in again, cussing myself, and it was another couple of minutes until I was on the dock with the bow line tied off. No hurry, I told myself, you know there's no hurry — but the urgency remained strong in me just the same. I ran along the dock, dragging the .38 out of my jacket, then up along the side of the A-frame and around to the front.

No Chrysler. Long gone by now.

I started toward the front door, but what the hell good would a check inside do me? Latimer wouldn't have left anything useful behind, and enough time had been wasted already. I ran back to the dock, untied the skiff. The outboard cooperated again; I went on a beeline to Judson's.

Marian stood waiting on the dock, as I'd expected she would be. Mack Judson was with her. They both hurried down as I powered in alongside the gas pumps, and Judson held the skiff steady as I clambered out. The tightness around his mouth told me he knew what was going on — as much as Marian knew, anyway. He had nothing to say, and that was good because after the one glance at him, I gave all my attention to her.

She was drawn about as tight as you can get, the way a cocked crossbow is drawn tight. I didn't touch her; I was afraid that if I did it would trigger her in some way. Not into hysterics — she was not the type — but into some other reaction that I would not know how to cope with.

She said between her teeth, "Where's Chuck?"

"Marian . . ."

"Where is he? Where's my son?"

"I don't know. He wasn't at Chuck's Hole."

"Not at Latimer's cottage, either. I saw you stop there before you came here."

Latimer, she'd said. Not Strayhorn.

My expression must have told her what I was thinking. She said, "I made Pat tell me, all of it. Latimer has Chuck, hasn't he. Don't lie to me. He has my son."

"It looks that way. Your boat's tied at his dock and his car's gone."

She squeezed her eyes shut, popped them open again. And made a fist and slugged me in the chest, hard enough to hurt. It was a gesture of rage and frustration, but not one directed at me personally, even if it was deserved that way. She needed to lash out at something, somebody, and I was handy; she hardly seemed aware that she'd done it. It would have been all right with me if she'd belted me again, knocked me flat on my ass and then added a few kicks for good measure.

Judson said, "I think I saw his car go by

about six-fifteen, six-twenty. I was getting some firewood and I caught a quick glimpse. Didn't notice if there was anybody in the car with him."

I glanced at my watch. A few minutes past eight-thirty. "Little better than two hours ago," I said, and thought but didn't say: They could be in Nevada by now, anywhere within a hundred-and-fifty-mile radius.

"The law ought to be here any minute," Judson said. "Sheriff Rideout can put out . . . what's it called? All points bulletin?"

"There's already one out on Latimer. We'll need a two-state bulletin on the kidnapping, and the FBI has to be notified. Pat can get that done faster than the sheriff. He's got to be told in any case."

"Use the phone in my cabin. Rita's there, she can look after Marian —"

"I don't need looking after," Marian said. She sounded better, back off the edge; the punch she'd thrown had taken some of the quivering tension out of her. "Where would he take Chuck?" she asked me.

"No idea."

"*Why* did he take him? Why . . . kidnap . . ."

I had a couple of notions about that, but I was not about to get into them with her. I let her have a half-truth instead: "No telling

216

what's in the head of a man like Latimer."

"If he hates Pat so much . . ." She let the rest of it trail off. I could feel the shudder that went through her. At least one of the notions had crossed her mind, too.

I had her arm now, and the three of us were moving off the dock. There was nobody else around. Except for Rita Judson we were the only ones who knew what was about to go down here, but that would change as soon as the sheriff's contingent showed up. They'd come in force; there was no other way for county law to respond to the presence of a suspected serial bomber, an armed boobytrap, and the imminent helicopter arrival of a bomb squad.

Judson said awkwardly, "The boy'll be all right, Marian. You got to believe that. He'll be back to you safe and sound."

Hollow words, as heavy as stones dropped in the bright morning. Marian didn't respond to them, and neither did I.

At the cabin Judson led us into the kitchen where their phone was. Rita tried to steer Marian into another room, but she wasn't having any of that. She stayed close beside me, her fingers digging into my arm.

I asked her, "Pat say he'd be waiting at home?"

"Yes. For one of us to call about Chuck."

She read the number off to me and I made the call. Dixon must have been sitting on the phone; his voice said "Yes?" a fraction of a second after the first circuit ring sounded. I explained the situation, straight and fast and in as emotionless a tone as I could muster.

Long silence. Coming to terms with it, I thought, getting himself in hand. When he finally spoke, his voice was hard, raspy. "If I have the chance," he said, "I'll make Latimer pay for this. I'll make him pay in blood."

"Pat —"

"I'm all right," he said.

"You sure?"

"I'm all right. County sheriff get there yet?"

"Not yet. Any minute."

"You haven't called his office, notified them about the . . . about Chuck?"

"I just got back. You're the first call."

"Keep it that way. I'll take care of it."

"Two-state APB, and the FBI —"

"You don't have to tell me what to do."

"Easy, Pat."

"Sure, easy. What kind of car is Latimer driving?"

"Ten-year-old Chrysler LeBaron. Tan, pretty beat up."

"License number?"

I gave it to him from memory.

"Okay," he said. Then he said, "Marian? Does she know?"

"Yeah. She's right here, I'll put her on —"

"No. Wait . . . all right, let me talk to her. But you get her out of there as soon as you can. Bring her back to the city."

"Your place?"

"No. The Doyles'. She'll give you the address."

"Where'll you be?"

"Don't know yet. Maybe here, maybe the D.A.'s office."

"What about the bomb squad?"

"On their way from Sacramento."

"Yeah, I figured that. I meant the SFPD bomb unit. For the sweep of your house."

"Oh . . . been and gone. They didn't find anything."

"Then why don't I just bring Marian home?"

"Goddamn it, do what I tell you!" Sharp, borderline savage. "The Doyles', understand? Now put her on."

I handed her the receiver, went out of the kitchen to give her some privacy. Both Judsons followed me, but I had nothing to say to them just then and I kept on going, outside. I stood in the direct sunlight, waiting for its heat to warm me. It didn't happen; I could not even feel it on the bunched skin of my neck and shoulders.

No way the SFPD bomb squad could have swept his house since the last time we talked, I was thinking. They're damned thorough normally and they'd be extra careful in the case of a public official. Dixon called them off. Why, when there's still a chance, however slight, that Latimer set a backup boobytrap there? Why doesn't he want Marian home?

Only one explanation I could think of. And I didn't like anything about it.

This one: Latimer had contacted him by phone sometime between Marian's call and mine just now, told him he had the boy. Which meant Latimer was still fixated on finishing his vendetta and was using Chuck as a lever to force a meeting with Dixon. And Pat, the damn fool, was letting himself be pried; believing he could work a trade, probably — his life for his son's — with a lunatic who had already murdered three people.

14

By nine-thirty Deep Mountain Lake looked like a place under siege.

The first county law arrived in a four-car caravan, seven minutes after I talked to Dixon and two minutes after I finished stowing the .38 Colt Bodyguard inside my car; there was no longer any reason for me to be packing heat, and it's never a good idea, anyway, for a private detective to walk around armed in the midst of an official crisis situation. Another green-and-white cruiser showed up shortly afterward, and two more within ten minutes of that one. None of them came with sirens or flashers, but the sheer numbers alerted the local population and word spread fast.

The man in charge was Sheriff Ben Rideout, a lanky guy in his fifties with a military bearing and a quiet, no-nonsense manner. He was a little stiff with me at first, either because I was a stranger or because of what I did for a living, but he didn't hassle me and it wasn't long before my own professionalism eased things between us.

His first question to me was, "Where's Donald Latimer?"

"Gone. Since about six-fifteen this morning."

"So now we've got a fugitive. Why weren't we notified?"

"Just confirmed a few minutes ago. I called Pat Dixon and he's handling notification — county, state, and federal."

"Why call him for that?"

"Because Latimer's not alone," I said. "He's got Dixon's son with him." I laid out the basic details for him, nothing more. I was not sure yet what to do about my suspicions — the best way to handle the situation for Chuck's sake, for Pat's.

"Bad," Rideout said, "very bad. Not much we can do about that part of it now. Latimer won't still be hanging around Plumas County, that's for sure. What can you tell me about the explosive device in the Dixon cabin?"

"Not much. If he and I are right, it's wired into his tackle box and it's the frag type — fishhooks, lots of them, and Christ knows what else."

"Dynamite? Plastic explosive?"

"Not sure. Probably the same or similar to the previous two bombs in San Francisco —"

"Black powder," one of the other officers said. The second-in-command, a youngish lieutenant named Dewers.

"Right, black powder."

"How much pucker power?" Rideout asked me.

"Again, probably along the lines of the other two. A concentrated load, designed to do the most damage to the person who triggers it."

"So not enough to blow up the entire cabin. Or any of the neighboring cabins, maybe set off a forest fire."

"Doubtful, judging from the size and weight of the box."

"Okay. That's pretty much what we were led to believe, but I wanted your take. You've seen and handled the thing, right?"

"Yeah," I said.

Rideout called to his driver, "Sam, what's the latest ETA on the Sacramento bomb unit?" Evidently his radio had a patch through to the incoming helicopter.

The driver checked, called back, "Thirty minutes."

"We better get a move on."

He deployed his officers, a dozen men and two women. One unit to a meadow a third of a mile east of the lake to wait for the chopper; I heard Judson say that the meadow had been used once before, a few years back, by a medivac helicopter to bring out a boating accident victim. Two units to keep order at the resort, which was already attracting summer residents and guests like flies swarming to spoiled meat. Four units to evacuate and secure the danger zone — all the cottages between the resort and the Dixon cabin, in order to ensure a clear road, and any occupied cottages within a thousand yards west of the Dixons'. Rideout and Dewers would make sure nobody got anywhere near the device until the bomb squad arrived. The sheriff gave me the option of going along with them and I took it. It was better than hanging and rattling at the resort.

I sat in the backseat of the sheriff's cruiser. Faces in the parking lot and along the road stared in at me as we moved out, the blank, hostile stares citizens always give prisoners. I felt like one, sitting there behind the thick mesh screen that separated front and rear seats. Guilt, mainly — and the kind of trapped feeling you get when you're at the mercy of others. I kept thinking that I ought to say something to Rideout about a possible contact between Latimer and Dixon, and I kept not doing it. It was only conjecture on my part, for one thing. And more important, I wasn't convinced I had a moral right to take that step. Chuck was Dixon's son — and I couldn't even be sure of what I'd do if the boy were mine.

When we passed the green-shingled cottage Latimer had occupied, I roused myself long enough to point it out to the sheriff. He nodded without turning his head. "We'll check it out later. First things first."

Nobody was hanging around in the immediate vicinity of the Dixon cabin. That helped the evacuation and area-securing process move along quickly and smoothly. The Plumas County deputies were well trained; they had bystanders moved out to Judson's or safe behind police lines and the road blocked off and empty by the time we heard the chopper coming in to the east.

I stood with Dewers and a couple of the other officers behind the yellow-tape barrier on the cabin's east side, waiting for the bomb techs to be ferried in from the landing site. Every time I looked at the cabin it was as though I had X-ray vision: I could see that tackle box sitting there on the floor against the wall. I could feel the weight of it, a kind of ghost-prickle on my fingers, and the careless swing of it against my leg as I walked, and the slight jarring way in which I'd set it down. Any of those movements could have initiated it. The memory, and the thought that neither Chuck nor I would have known what hit us, summoned up fresh beads of sweat.

It took about fifteen minutes for the two transport cruisers to arrive. They slid past the barrier, rolled to a stop in front of the cabin. From what I could see at the distance, there were three techs and they were traveling light from necessity. Bomb disarmament these days is a highly sophisticated process, as I'd learned from a former SFPD technician I'd gotten to know in the course of an investigation. Electronic gadgetry played a big role in it; so did such state-of-the-art equipment as remote-controlled and track-driven robots outfitted with X rays and TV cameras, a thing called a "disruptor" that shoots water or slugs with pinpoint accuracy to break apart a bomb's circuitry, and total containment vessels inside of which even a high-charge device can be safely detonated.

But apparatus like that is bulky, made and outfitted for ground transport. These techs had to utilize portable equipment because of a helicopter's limited cargo capacity; what they unloaded from the cruisers, as near as I could tell, included a small X-ray machine and both body armor and a Galt bomb suit, an outfit made by the British that resembles a marine diving suit — heavy helmet and breastplate, an antiblast shield for the face. So this crew would be handling Latimer's tackle-box boobytrap the old-fashioned way, up close and deadly. They'd "surgically" disable it if they could, to keep everything intact so it could be used as evidence in court. More likely they'd decide the safest method was to carefully dump the thing in the lake. Immersion in water will neutralize most explosive devices, among them the kinds built with black powder.

Once the techs were ready to enter the cabin, the deputies in the cruisers drove out of harm's way; so did Rideout, who'd gone up there to confer with the squad commander. He brought an order to move everybody even farther back, which put us around a bend in the road and out of viewing range. Just as well. I did not care to be watching if anything happened.

"Now we wait," Rideout said when we were reestablished. "And it's going to be a while."

Dewers said, "Waiting is one of my least favorite activities. How about if Sam and I go check out Latimer's cottage?"

"Okay, do it."

I said, "All right if I go along? I'm not

much good at waiting, either." Understatement. I was so keyed up I felt ready to jump out of my skin.

Rideout and the lieutenant exchanged glances. Dewers shrugged and said, "No objection. He's been around Latimer. Might be evidence there that'll mean something to him but wouldn't to us."

We piled into Dewers' cruiser, the sheriff's driver, Sam, behind the wheel and me in the prisoner's seat again. None of us had any comment to make until we were rolling. Then, on impulse, I leaned forward and said to Dewers, "Mind if I ask a favor?"

"Well, you can ask."

"Check with your dispatcher, see what's on the air about Latimer."

"If there was any news on him or the boy, we'd have been notified."

"I'd just like to know for sure that both state and federal agencies have word on the kidnapping."

"Bound to, by now." He slid around on the seat and frowned at me through the mesh. "Unless you think there's some reason Dixon didn't follow through."

Good man, this Dewers. Sharp. I said, hedging, "I'm just edgy, that's all. Would you check?"

He turned front again, reached for the

radio handset. I listened to him and to the crackly voice of the Quincy dispatcher. And what I heard made me even more antsy.

"The APB on Latimer's still in effect," the dispatcher said, "but there's nothing out on a kidnapping. We thought you had the perp in custody or contained up there. We've been waiting for a communication."

Oversight glitch by Rideout or Dewers; the lieutenant didn't respond to it. He said, "You sure there's nothing on the kidnap?"

"Affirmative, Lieutenant."

"Contact Sacramento CID, tell them that Latimer and the Dixon boy have been missing since six-fifteen this A.M. Tell them . . . Wait a minute." Dewers swiveled his head. "What kind of vehicle is Latimer driving?"

I told him, added the license number.

"Description of the boy?"

I gave him that in one sentence.

He relayed the information, then told the dispatcher to ask Sacramento CID if they'd heard anything from Dixon or the San Francisco D.A.'s office since his call for the bomb squad. "Get back to me as soon as you can," he said, and signed off, and swung around to look at me again. "All right, what's going on with Dixon?"

"I wish I knew."

"You must have some idea."

I hesitated. My suspicions had a solid basis now, but there was still the moral dilemma. And that was a hurdle I couldn't seem to get past, at least not until I talked to Marian. I said, "Stress, maybe. Lot of pressure on him."

"He's not a boozer, is he?"

"Not the kind you mean, no."

Dewers seemed about to make another suggestion — the right one, like as not — but our arrival at Latimer's rented A-frame kept him from voicing it. All he said as we turned down the driveway was, "We'll get to the bottom of this."

Sam parked alongside the dogwood bushes. Dewers told him to wait for the dispatcher to radio back, then got out and released me. It seemed too quiet here, almost preternaturally so, after all the hubbub around the Dixon cabin. The pine-sweet air felt skimpy in my lungs, as if there wasn't enough oxygen in it.

"If the front door's locked," Dewers said, "we'll each take a side and check other doors and windows. If everything's locked, then we'll break in. In any case, I'll go in first, alone, and see what's what. Clear?"

"Clear."

"Stay here until I give you a yell."

I nodded, and he went up onto the platform porch. He didn't draw the .357 Magnum holstered at his side, but he closed fingers around the handle as he reached out with his other hand to try the latch. It wasn't locked. I saw him ease the door open partway, then all the way —

The blast, as concussively loud as a small bomb, blew him backward and off his feet. He hit the planks on hips and shoulders, bounced, skidded. I'd been leaning against the cruiser's rear fender; I was off it and running toward him before the echoes faded and he came to rest in a twisted back sprawl. Behind me I heard the cruiser's door slap open, Sam yell something in a stricken voice. I slowed then, but not because of him.

Dewers wasn't moving; he'd never move again. His chest was a gaping red-black ruin, little wisps of grayish vapor rising from it, blood spattered up over his arms and face, blood slicking the boards where he'd skidded. More vapor came dribbling out through the open cabin door.

My stomach heaved; I had to turn away to keep my gorge down. Sam ran up and I heard him say, "Oh Jesus!" with as much awed reverence as a priest in prayer. I took a couple of loose steps away from the body, to where I could look in through the doorway.

Two chairs, both toppled. Hand clamps on them and on the floor. Lengths of string and thin wire, one piece of wire attached to the inside of the doorknob, another to the trigger of the weapon that had recoiled halfway across the room. Rigged to fire at point-blank range, after the Magnum shell had first been reloaded with black powder. The room was smoky and stank of cordite.

Now I knew why Latimer had stolen the Mossberg .410 shotgun.

I knew something else, too, standing there shaking with sickness and fury. Knew it beyond any doubt.

This boobytrap had been meant for me.

15

They kept me on the scene for more than half an hour. It could have been much longer, but after the first rush and barrage of questions from a grim and shaken Sheriff Rideout they lost interest in me. They swarmed over the cottage, looking for any pieces of Latimer that he might've left behind. He was their focus now; even the movements of the bomb squad had become secondary to the brutal slaying of one of their own.

I went down by the lake, where I would not have to look at the blanket-shrouded body of Lieutenant Dewers, and waited restlessly for them to let me go back to the resort. Inside I was still seething and strung tight. I hadn't told Rideout about Dixon's failure to put out state and federal warrants on Latimer; neither had Sam, as far as I knew. For the time being, that fact had gotten lost in the aftermath of Dewers's violent death. I hoped it would stay lost until I could talk to Marian, try to get her husband on the phone — make my decision one way or the other.

The moral issue was only part of it now.

The shotgun boobytrap and Dewers's death had made it personal. Latimer had almost ended my life twice in two days, once inadvertently and once with premeditation. That shotgun charge had been intended for me, all right. I was supposed to be the one lying up there with his chest torn to bloody shreds. He'd hated me since our first meeting, and never mind that the reasons were irrational. Feared me, too, because of who and what I was. So he'd added me to his hit list. Figured I'd be the first to come snooping around his cottage when I found him and Chuck gone, and built his boobytrap accordingly. He'd almost guessed right, too; I'd come close to opening the front door myself earlier. Close.

The only reason I was still alive was luck and his psychosis. He'd had plenty of opportunity to take me out with a gun or knife or blunt instrument, but he preferred to do his killing at a distance, with detachment and methodical prearrangement and no threat to himself. The coward's way. Nils Ostergaard must've been an unavoidable necessity. And it must've bothered the hell out of him when it was done.

I stared out at the lake, thinking that I hated Latimer right now more than he could possibly hate me. That I'd like nothing better than an active role in bringing him down before he harmed Pat or Chuck or anyone else; how good it would feel to get close enough to spit in his face. But that was as far as it went. There was no desire for violence in what I felt, just a cold determination that was every bit as personal as a blood vendetta. Violence all around me, aimed at me, but none of it had penetrated. I was like a chunk of stone inside a protective force field: it couldn't hurt me or turn me into an instrument of violence myself. What I'd thought and felt out at Chuck's Hole yesterday morning was not a situational reaction but an absolute truth. I was all through with killing or hurting any living thing, except as a last line of self-defense. It was simply not in me anymore to become an avenger, or even a shadow of one.

So I sat there and hated Latimer in my own way and waited for somebody to come and either question me some more or set me free. It wasn't Rideout but a uniformed deputy who finally walked down, which told me even before he spoke that they were through with me for the time being. "Sheriff says for you to go on back to the resort," he said. He didn't offer to drive me; neither did anyone else. That was all right, too. Physical activity was what I needed at the moment, a way to work off some of the tension.

When I reached Judson's I found things to be pretty quiet. Several cars were in evidence, a county cruiser with two officers inside blocking the road, but most of the residents and guests seemed to be jammed into the cafe. Three stood in front of the grocery half, one of them Fred Dyce; he glanced my way and then turned aside — embarrassed about last night, maybe, if he even remembered what'd happened. The quiet wouldn't last long, I thought. Just until the media started showing up and the news about Latimer and the kidnapping and Dewers's death got spread around. Then we'd have Carnival. That was as certain as death itself.

I went straight to the Judsons' A-frame, and Rita opened up and let me in. Marian stood waiting in the living room, her face pale but otherwise composed.

"Have they finished with the bomb?" she asked.

"Not yet. Anything from Pat?"

"No, not since you left."

"I'm going to try calling him. Then you and I need to talk."

I shut myself in the kitchen, punched out the Dixons' home number. Fifteen rings, no answer. I called the D.A.'s office and talked briefly to one of the other A.D.A.s; Pat wasn't there, hadn't been there all day and hadn't reported in since he'd put through the request for the Sacramento bomb squad.

Bad, as bad as I'd feared. But not hopeless yet.

What happened next was up to Marian.

I got her alone in the Judsons' bedroom and laid it out for her. All of it, except for what had happened to Dewers; her defenses were fragile enough without that blow and its implications. At one point she sat heavily on the nearest twin bed, as if her legs had gone shaky on her. Otherwise she took it as well as anybody could. No tears, no emotional reaction of any kind. She just sat there, looking up at me out of wide, pained eyes.

"What are we going to do?" she said.

"Right now, the choice is yours."

"Mine? I don't understand."

"There are two ways we can handle this," I said. "You'll have to choose which one, and quickly. Pat's your husband, Chuck's your son."

"Yes," she said. "All right."

"The first way, I tell Sheriff Rideout everything I've just told you. We put everything in official hands, take ourselves out of it completely."

"Isn't that the right thing to do?"

"It's the approved thing. I haven't done it yet because it wasn't my place. I don't feel I can take the responsibility."

"Thank you for that. Go on."

"The authorities have manpower, resources, experience. But it takes time for them to mobilize, interact with one another, and the information that Latimer is at large with your son was given to them only a short while ago. At any time, now that word is out, an officer somewhere could spot Latimer's car and do what's necessary to free Chuck. If that happens, it'll happen no matter what we do. More likely, Latimer will be able to get to where he's going without interference, if he hasn't already. In any case, official wheels are turning, and once they turn fast enough, whether or not we tell anybody about Pat, bunches of state cops and FBI agents are going to start showing up with questions and agendas."

"You mean . . . here?"

"Here, yes, if this is where you are."

"Are you telling me we won't be able to leave?"

"It's unlikely Rideout would let us go anywhere until the higher-ups arrive. That's the way it's done; the feds in particular want the nearest responsible relative in a kidnapping — you — to be close at hand in the event something happens. They'll let you go home eventually, but not today unless Latimer and Chuck are found. You'll have to spend the night here or in Quincy or maybe in Sacramento, wherever they decide is best, and you won't have much privacy."

"My God," Marian said, "I don't want that, I couldn't stand that. I want to be at home if Pat or Chuck . . . that's the only place where I can . . ." She seemed to realize she was starting to ramble. She bit her lower lip, hard, maybe hard enough to draw blood. Using the pain as a way to calm herself, I thought; it was something I'd done myself once or twice. When she spoke again, the frantic edge was gone from her voice. "What's the other alternative?"

"We take a partial hands-on position for the time being. Don't tell the sheriff anything — I go to him and ask permission to drive you back to the city. If nothing has come through on Latimer's whereabouts, or any official requests to detain either of us, I think he'll agree to it. As things stand now, he has no real reason to keep us here."

"Then what? Once we get to the city?"

"We go to your home. And pray Pat's still there."

"I don't . . . you said he didn't answer. . . ."

"Not answering the phone doesn't mean he's not there. It could be Latimer's holed up between here and San Francisco and Pat's gone to meet him. But it could also be that Latimer's headed for a place in or near the city. Not your house; I doubt he'd risk that. Maybe wherever he lived before he came to Deep Mountain Lake. If that's the case, he's barely had enough time to reach the Bay Area. And he's methodical, a planner — he doesn't do anything on the spur of the moment unless he has no other option. The odds are that whatever he's planning, he'll need time to set it up." I thought but didn't add: And with his sadistic streak, he'd get a bang out of letting Pat stew and sweat for a few hours, possibly a lot of hours.

Marian did the lip-biting thing again. "If you're right . . . then Pat's still home?"

"If I'm right."

"Why wouldn't he answer the phone?"

"He wouldn't want to talk to anyone but Latimer, not even you. And it could be Latimer gave him a specific time to expect another call. We can get there by six or

240

six-thirty, if we're on the road in the next half hour or so. That might be soon enough."

"You could just call Al Ybarra or Dave Maccerone, couldn't you? They could go to the house, and if Pat's there . . ."

"If he's there, he's forted in. He wouldn't open up for anybody and there'd be no grounds for forcible entry. Even if they did talk to him, Pat wouldn't be likely to admit what he intends to do."

"No. No, he wouldn't. He can be very stubborn when his mind is made up."

"They could watch the house, follow him when he leaves, but that's an iffy proposition. And if Pat shows up for his meeting with Latimer dragging a police tail . . . well, anything might happen."

There was a little silence before she said, "I don't think he'd listen to me, either."

"You'd have a better chance than anyone else — you and me together. You must have some influence over him where Chuck is concerned."

"Some, yes . . . Oh God, I don't know what's best. I just don't know!"

"Nobody knows, Marian. It's all gray area, no matter which way you turn."

"Would Latimer . . . do you think he'd . . . hurt a child?"

"The honest truth? He's capable of it."

"Pat must feel the same. He must believe that trying to . . . trade . . . is the only way to save Chuck's life."

"Probably, but he's wrong. It's not the only way. And you can't barter with a lunatic, no matter how much you want to believe otherwise. If he puts himself in Latimer's hands —"

"He'll die and Chuck will die. That's what you're saying. Both of them will die."

"There's a strong chance of it, yes."

"You could be wrong. . . ."

"I could be. If Pat does meet Latimer, I hope to God I am. The point I'm trying to make is that it's a miserable situation any way you look at it and anything can happen, good or bad, no matter what you decide or what anybody does."

She gave her head a loose, wobbly shake. "If we go to the city . . . if Pat isn't home . . . what then?"

"We notify the authorities. Immediately. But that's getting ahead of ourselves. There are other things we can do even before we get to the city. Monitor the manhunt situation, for one, so we'll know right away if there are any new developments. That can be done through my assistant, Tamara Corbin."

"I don't know," Marian said again. "I can't make up my mind, I can't seem to think straight. . . ."

"I understand. Believe me, I do." I touched her arm, gently; her muscles seemed to twitch under my fingers. "Suppose I give you a few minutes? I'll go talk to Sheriff Rideout, see if he'll even allow us to leave —"

"No. No, I don't want to just sit here, I can't stand any more sitting and waiting." Abruptly she got to her feet. "It's a choice between passive and active, isn't it? Doing something or doing nothing."

"In a sense."

"All right. I'll go with you, and after you find out if we can leave . . . then I'll decide."

We left the A-frame, cut behind the main resort building toward where the county cruiser was parked blocking the road. Plenty of noise came from inside the cafe, voices rising and falling in an excited babble. From the snatches I could make out, they were all talking about the boobytrap bomb and the kidnapping, which meant that the first of the media — reporters from the Quincy area, probably — had arrived and spread the word. News of Dewers's death hadn't been made public yet; Rideout would be keeping the lid on tight until the lieutenant's next of kin could be notified and the bomb squad finished their work.

Marian walked close beside me, clinging to my arm, her hip touching mine now and then. Her trust in me made me feel guilty again. I wondered if I hadn't manipulated her, eased her in the direction I wanted her to go. I'd tried to present both options in a neutral fashion, but I couldn't deny there'd been a subtle bias. Bad enough the way things were, with the load I was already carrying; if she went the way I wanted and something happened to Pat or the boy or both of them . . .

Cut it out, I told myself. You told her the truth, subtle bias or not. A child in the hands of a madman is the worst kind of pressure situation there is and there are no hard and fast rules because nothing's predictable, no course you take is completely right or safe. The real fault lies with the madman, no one else. All you can do is make your choices and hope they're the right ones — trust your instincts and your experience, put your faith in God or fate or whatever you happen to believe in. If it turns out badly, you die a little. If it turns out well, it's like a rebirth. Either way, you have to accept it.

We reached the cruiser without any attention being paid to us from the cafe. One officer sat inside, an older guy with a salt-and-pepper mustache; his partner was down the road a ways, talking to a couple of men I didn't recognize. I told him who I was, who Marian was, and that I needed to speak briefly with Sheriff Rideout. Yes, it was important. Would he call him on the radio?

He was the right man to have approached; he did what I asked without much protest. Rideout wasn't immediately available. It took about five minutes before he radioed back.

I said, when I had the receiver, "I'd like permission to drive Mrs. Dixon back to San Francisco so she can be with her husband."

Staticky pause. At length he said, "There'll be people who want to talk to her."

"I know. They can do that with her at home, can't they?"

"I suppose so."

"I can have her there by six, six-thirty."

"What about you? Where can you be reached?"

"At my home tonight, at my office tomorrow. The numbers and addresses are listed."

"You're a witness," Rideout said. "We

245

may need you to sign a written statement."

"I can do that by mail or fax. But if it's necessary for me to come back up here, for any reason, you have my word that I'll cooperate."

Another staticky pause. His mike was open; I heard him say to somebody, "Okay, right. It's about time they decided to dump that goddamn thing in the lake." Then, to me again, "All right. You can go."

I looked at Marian. She nodded; she'd made up her mind — firm. "Can we leave right away?" I asked Rideout.

"Just make sure you take Mrs. Dixon straight home."

"As fast as I can get her there safely."

I returned the mike to the deputy, walked Marian back toward the Judsons' A-frame. "You're sure this is what you want to do?" I asked her.

"I'm sure. Yes."

"Okay. Get whatever you want to take along and wait for me in the cabin. I'll come get you pretty quick."

"Where are you going?"

"To talk to somebody. An idea I have. I won't be more than ten minutes."

I veered around to the front of the main resort building and went into the cafe. Hal Cantrell was where I figured he'd be, at the bar — chattering to two other guys, a bottle of beer in his hand and an excited gleam in his eye. Enjoying himself. One of the blood-and-disaster freaks. Well, maybe I could turn that to our advantage if I handled him right.

It took a little doing to pry him away from his audience and get him outside and off to where we had some privacy. I managed it by whispering to him that I needed a favor, an important favor, and that he was the only one who could help me with it.

"So," he said when we were alone, "what's this favor?"

"Make a couple of phone calls for me."

"Phone calls? Who to?"

"Your real-estate office, first. Have some-body run a rental listings check — all the brokers county wide — and find out if Donald Latimer rented a house or apart-ment in the Half Moon Bay area at any time in the past month to six weeks. Under his own name or as Jacob Strayhorn. That's possible, isn't it?"

"Possible, sure, but — Hey, why Half Moon Bay?"

"Chance he lived there before he came up here."

"Not Stockton, huh?"

"Not Stockton."

247

"Why do you care if he lived in Half Moon Bay?"

"Never mind why. Will you do it?"

His mouth quirked in a sly, boozy little grin. "What's in it for me?"

"A hundred bucks, cash. And some free publicity if it turns out to be useful information that helps nail Latimer."

"Yeah? You think it will?"

"Pretty good chance," I lied.

"Well, I always did like to see my name in the papers. Who's the other call to?"

"Me. My car phone as soon as you get the information."

"You leaving here?"

"Driving Mrs. Dixon back to San Francisco." I dragged my wallet out. I'd brought plenty of cash along, the way you do on vacations; I picked out five twenties, but I didn't let him have the money yet. "One other thing. This is just between you and me. Don't discuss it with anyone, and I mean anyone, for twenty-four hours."

"Law included?"

"The law included. If you do, you won't like what I have to say to the media about your cooperation."

Cantrell shrugged. "A deal's a deal with me," he said. Now he was serious; the grin was gone. "I'll take your money" — he plucked the twenties out of my fingers — "but that's not the real reason I'm going along. Not for any glory, either."

"No, huh?"

"No. For the woman and her kid. I got kids of my own, you know."

"I'll bet you're a good father."

The sarcasm was lost on him. "Better'n most."

"And a good citizen."

"Try to be," he said, and he even managed to sound sincere. If he didn't believe it now, he'd manage to talk himself into it before long. He was just that variety of self-serving, self-deluded asshole.

I took him with me to the Judsons' cabin, told Rita what he was going to do without getting into specifics and asked her to please make sure her phone stayed free until he had the information I was after. She said she would and she didn't ask questions. I wrote my car phone number on a piece of notepaper, handed it to Cantrell. In return, he gave me a mock salute and went off with Rita to the kitchen.

Marian was ready. I hustled her out of there, across the lot to where she'd parked my car. We were just getting inside when a couple of guys came running toward us, one with a camera in his hand, the other shouting, "Hey! Hey, wait a minute!" Reporters. I told Marian to lock her door, locked mine, fired up the engine as the two guys reached the car and the shouter started banging on the window glass. I managed not to do him any damage as I drove us away.

16

The first thing I did when we cleared the immediate area was to try calling Tamara on the car phone. No good; I couldn't get through a wall of static. I'd had trouble with the mobile unit before in mountainous terrain, particularly bad-weather or windy days, and during the past hour or so a high, sharp wind had begun to blow up here. Kerry kept telling me to get the thing replaced with a more sophisticated cell phone and I kept putting it off like the bullheaded procrastinator she said I was. Damn car was going in for a new unit first of next week.

I drove too fast along the rough road, Marian sitting rigidly beside me, staring straight ahead and not making a sound even when a bump or pothole bounced us around like clay figures in a box. She didn't want conversation right now and that was fine with me. There was plenty of time — between five and six long hours — for what talking we had left to do.

We cleared the last sheriff's roadblock at the Bucks Lake Road intersection, began to wind down to lower elevations. I tried the phone again as we neared Quincy. Still staticky, but I could make out circuit rings through the crackle, which meant Tamara and I could hear each other. I stayed on until she answered, and it was all right as long as both of us spoke loudly and distinctly.

"Been hoping you'd call," she said. "Bombs, kidnapping — man, shit does happen when you're around."

"Yeah. How'd you hear about it?"

"Joe DeFalco. Called a while ago, said soon as he got word what was going down up there he knew you were involved."

"What'd you tell him?"

Mutter, mutter wrapped in static.

"Say that again. Louder."

"Told him everything I know — nothing much. Where're you?"

I told her that and who was with me and where we were going; the rest could wait until later. "What I need," I said then, "is for you to keep on top of the situation with Latimer. I don't mean media reports, I mean an official pipeline — I want to know immediately if and when anything breaks over the next five hours. Can do?"

Static. Then, ". . . be no problem. Felicia owes me one."

Felicia was Felicia Jackson, a friend of

Tamara's who worked in the SFPD's communications department. Tamara never ceased to amaze me, not only with her computer skills but in other ways; in a few short months she'd made personal contacts in strategic places that it would've taken me years to establish.

"Any news," I said, "even if it's unconfirmed."

"You got it."

Into Quincy, out of it again rolling southeast on Highway 70. Traffic was fairly light; I let the speedometer needle ease up over seventy and hang there. My instinct was to bear down even harder, but I was afraid to run the risk of accident or attracting the attention of the Highway Patrol. There were quite a few HP patrols in the Sierras during summer months and they weren't inclined to be forgiving of speeders.

Marian still had nothing to say. I glanced over at her now and then and her position didn't change; she seemed almost catatonic, lost deep inside herself. The inside of my head was not a good place to be right now; the inside of her head, I thought, must be three times as bleak and haunted.

We were coming up on a wide place in the road called Cromberg when the phone buzzed. I yanked the receiver out of its cradle, almost dropped it in my haste to get the line open.

Cantrell. And a static-free connection. I heard him loud and clear when he said, "You're out of luck."

"What does that mean?"

"No rentals in the Half Moon Bay area by Donald Latimer or Jacob Strayhorn."

"Your office is sure of that?"

"Positive. I even had my girl check back two full months, just in case."

"How wide an area did she cover?"

"All of San Mateo County."

"All right. Listen, call her back and have her check Santa Cruz County rentals. And if that's a dead end . . . a list of all the rentals by a single male in the Half Moon Bay area over the past six weeks. He could've used another name."

"You don't want much for your hundred bucks."

"I thought you weren't doing this for the money. Or the publicity."

". . . Okay, right. But what good's a list going to do you? Rental could be in a man's name only, but he's taking the place for his family, girlfriend, boyfriend, whatever. Bound to be a lot of names in any case, this time of year."

"We can narrow it down. Chances are he

wouldn't have much money to spend, and he'd have to pay in cash. And his references would be shaky at best."

"Have to be a low-end property," Cantrell said musingly. "A dog listing that some agent'd be so anxious to unload, he wouldn't bother to check references. I don't operate that way, but there're some in the business who do."

Oh, sure, you're not one of them. I said, "Anything that looks promising, have your office person call the agent and find out if the renter's description matches Latimer's."

"Fat chance. He looks like half the white guys on the street these days. Besides, that's liable to take all afternoon."

"You planning on going anywhere?"

"No, but I'm tired of sitting around, away from all the action."

"I feel for you. But not half as much as I feel for the Dixons."

"Yeah, all right, I hear you. But this is the end of it."

"One way or the other," I said.

If he heard that, he didn't respond to it. Noise had started up in the background, voices chattering words I couldn't make out. After about fifteen seconds, Cantrell said, "Mack just came in. Looks like the bomb squad's finally finished and on their way out of here. Bomb didn't blow up, at least there wasn't any big boom, but something must've happened. Mack said an ambulance just went tearing out that way."

I let all of that pass. "Call your office. Don't let us down, Cantrell."

"Count on me, don't worry."

Yeah. The lid was coming off the shotgun slaying of Lieutenant Dewers; once it was all the way off, the excitement level at Deep Mountain Lake would climb again. That and the impending media swarm would lure Cantrell like flame lures bugs. If his "girl" had gotten back to him before then, I'd get another call from him. If not, I'd just had my last conversation with the caring, reliable, and humanitarian Hal Cantrell.

Marian roused herself as I slid the phone receiver back into its cradle. She'd been listening to my end of the exchange, had figured out from that what I had Cantrell doing. She wanted to know how I knew Latimer had been living in the Half Moon Bay area. I told her about Nils Ostergaard's suspicions, the Safeway receipt I'd found in his truck.

"Latimer killed Nils, didn't he. It wasn't an accident."

"It looks that way. I think he caught Nils snooping around his cottage Sunday night and killed him there and then moved the body later."

"Poor Nils. My God." Then she asked, "Do you think it's possible Latimer took Chuck to Half Moon Bay?"

"Possible, yes."

"But not likely."

"As likely as any other possibility right now."

She didn't believe it. She fell silent again.

All right, I thought, so it's a long shot. What else do we have except long shots?

The miles rolled away and we were in Truckee shortly before three o'clock. I stopped on the outskirts for gas and something to put in my stomach. No food since last night and the tension had created a sour, burning pain under my breastbone. While the tank was filling I bought three packaged sandwiches and a couple of sodas in the station's convenience store. We were back on the road again in ten minutes, heading south on Interstate 80 five minutes after that.

Marian refused the sandwich I offered and I couldn't coax her into it. She did take one of the sodas. I washed a tasteless ham-and-cheese down, made myself eat a second sandwich, some kind of stale meat, on the theory that I needed to keep my own fuel level up; the food lay in my stomach in a hard glutinous mass and the carbonation in the soda gave me gas that I had difficulty controlling. Not that Marian would have noticed if I'd belched like a foghorn. She sat over tight against the passenger door, her head tilted back and her eyes closed, but she wasn't resting. The tension level in the car was as heavy as dead air in a vacuum.

Up and over Donner Summit, down past Emigrant Gap. I kept glancing at her, at the equally silent car phone. I wanted the thing to ring — and I didn't want it to ring. If it did and it was Tamara, it would probably be bad news.

Baxter, Colfax, Bowman, down toward Auburn. Running into more traffic now. And my gut was hurting again; the damn sandwiches seemed to have solidified down there, resisting all internal efforts at digestion.

Nothing from Tamara.

Nothing from Cantrell.

Auburn. Newcastle. Rocklin.

The dashboard clock: 4:05. My wristwatch: 4:08.

Roseville. Sacramento next.

And the phone went off.

Marian jumped, made a sound in her throat. I grabbed up the receiver, and

Tamara's voice said, "Felicia be just calling. There's news."

My breathing went a little funny. "Yes?"

"State cops found Latimer's car, the Chrysler."

"Where?"

"In some trees just outside the Truckee-Tahoe airport."

"You mean abandoned?"

"Since just after eight this morning," Tamara said. "No sign of him or the boy. What he did, they think, he parked the car there and walked into the airport and rented himself a car under his own name, then drove it back and picked up the kid and whatever else was in the Chrysler. Cleaned out when it be found. The man's got stones, you gotta give him that."

I was breathing all right again now. "What kind of car'd he rent?"

"New Toyota wagon. Dark blue. You want the license?"

"Go ahead."

She read off the number. Easy one; I wouldn't forget it.

"Not half as bad as it could be, right?" she said. "At least they didn't find any bodies."

"Yeah. Thanks, Tamara."

"Just be hoping I don't have to call you again."

Marian was a bent wall of stone beside me, her eyes like cave openings in its pale face. She said "Chuck?" as I replaced the handset, in the same fearful way she'd spoken his name on the Judsons' dock earlier.

"No word yet. Latimer switched cars at Truckee."

"Damn him." Savage whisper. "God-damn him."

I had nothing to say to that. We were both out of words again; the silence rebuilt, heavier than before. It was like something else in the car with us, an unclean thing crouched so close I could almost feel its prickly touch against my skin.

Rush-hour slowdown getting through Sacramento: more nerve-strain, more frustration. We finally broke loose on the western outskirts and I opened her up to near eighty, not much of a risk because the average traffic-flow speed on the long stretch between Sacramento and Fairfield is upward of seventy.

Five-twenty by the dashboard clock, and we were approaching the Carquinez Bridge, when the phone buzzed again.

Cantrell this time, to my relief. "I'd just about given up on you," I said.

"Yeah, well, you're lucky I'm a man of my

word. Some party going on up here."

And he'd already joined it, judging from the faint slur to his words. "I don't care about that. What've you got for me?"

"Four names, three towns on the coast — all low-end, short-term rentals. Took the girl until a few minutes ago to narrow it down that far. The original list —"

"Latimer's description match any of them?"

"No. She talked to three of the agents, they see dozens of people every day, none of 'em could remember back as far as a month, two months. Except one woman thought her client, the one in Montero Beach, was a fat guy in his sixties, but I know the agent, she drinks like a fish and you can't —"

"Names and addresses, Cantrell. Slowly."

Marian was alert beside me, and when she heard me say that she opened her purse, rummaged up a notebook and pencil. By then, Cantrell had run through the list once. I had him do it again, repeating everything aloud so Marian could write it down. Two of the names I asked him to spell so I could be certain we had them right.

Adam Greenspan, 21178 Coast Highway, Montero Beach.

Frank R. Slaydon, 1817 Seal Rock Road, Half Moon Bay.

K. M. Dusay, 850 Bluffside Drive, Half Moon Bay.

Howard Underwood, 1077 Cypress Hill, Pescadero.

"Any of the names mean anything to you?" Cantrell asked.

"No."

"Slaydon's a little like Strayhorn, huh?"

"A little. Okay, Cantrell. Thanks — we appreciate all your help."

"Don't forget where you got it," he said, and we both disconnected at the same time. For the last time.

Marian said, "If any of these men is Latimer . . . which one?"

"No idea yet, but if he was running true to form at the time, maybe we can find out."

I still had the receiver in my hand; I tapped the memory key for my office number. When Tamara came on, I said, "Now I've got something — computer work for you to do. Call up everything you can locate on the Latimer case five years ago, see if any of the four names I'm going to give you is connected in any way. This is urgent, Tamara."

"Be on it soon as we hang up. Names?" And when she had them, "You must be close to home by now. Where?"

"About fifteen minutes from the Bay Bridge," I said. "We should be at the Dixon

home before six-thirty if the traffic cooper-
ates. If you can't reach me on the car phone,
try the number there." I asked Marian for it,
rather than trust my memory, and relayed it
to Tamara.

During the evening rush most of the
bridge traffic is eastbound, out of the city;
since we were westbound we got across
without much slowdown. 101 South was
congested as usual. I stood it as long as I
could, got off and did some maneuvering on
side streets that brought us up into
Monterey Heights almost as fast as a more
direct route would have. It was 6:25 — and
Tamara hadn't called back — when I pulled
up in front of the Dixons' Spanish-style
house.

"I don't see Pat's car," Marian said.

"He'd have it in the garage if he's been
holed up all day."

"Oh God, please let him be here."

She wasn't talking to me, so I didn't
answer. She was out of the car before I was;
I took her arm to steady her as we climbed
the front steps, both of us stiff and sweaty
and drawn to the snapping point.

The front door was locked; Marian used
her key. And we went in to find out if God
was going to answer her prayer, give us at
least a partial reprieve.

FROM THE NOTEBOOKS OF
DONALD MICHAEL LATIMER

Tues., July 2 — 6:30 P.M.

Everything is ready.

All I have to do now is call Dixon. Not just yet, though, let the bastard sweat a while longer. I'm in no hurry, I don't want to be out of here and on the road to Indiana until after dark. Relax. Finish this entry, have a beer and the last can of chili. No hurry at all.

I just went in to check on the kid. He's quiet, but what else could he be, gagged and blindfolded and tied so tight to the bed he can't even move a finger? Pretty good kid, didn't give me any trouble all day. Too bad about him. But he's a Dixon, his old man's blood runs in his veins, so he won't be any great loss. Besides, there'll be a second or two when Mr. Prosecutor realizes too late what's about to happen to both him *and* his son, and I'd do anything for that second or two. Sweet! Sweeter than the original Plan, even if I don't get to see the big finish. Almost makes all the crap I had to go through at the lake worthwhile.

The one thing that would make it sweeter still was if fat old Mike Hammer was trussed up in there next to the kid.

Bothers me he's still alive. Shotgun surprise got somebody else instead, that's what the radio said a few minutes ago, some Plumas County cop. One less cop in the world, that's fine with me, but it should've been fatso. Well, I can fix him when I come back from Indiana.

If I come back from Indiana. If I even make it to Lawler Bluffs.

Every law enforcement agency in the country is looking for me by now and they'll double their efforts after tonight. Public Enemy No. 1. Hah! I really don't give a shit if they get me eventually, I've pretty much known all along I'm living on borrowed time and I'm resigned to it now. Rip Kathryn apart with marbles and bones before that happens and I'll die satisfied and happy. But even if I can't give her what she deserves, I'll have made sure Cotter and Turnbull and Dixon got theirs. I'll see the three of them in hell, at least.

I wonder if this is the way Bonnie and Clyde felt on their bank-robbing spree? My old pal, the Unabomber, on his way to the post office with another surprise package? The guy who took out all the lawyers with the assault rifle?

Steady, heady, ready. Happy as a lark.

Man, I feel *good!*

17

Dixon was there.

He heard us coming into the vestibule; footsteps made sharp clicking sounds on the tile floor, and there he was in the archway to a darkened living room, staring at us out of eyes that even at a distance looked like those of a hunted wolf's. His lean face was haggard, showing beard shadow. The white shirt and slacks he wore were both rumpled, pulled out of shape, as if he'd been sleeping in them.

Marian said "Pat!" in a choked voice and ran to him. He folded her against him, held her, but he was looking at me over her shoulder. An angry, desperate look.

After a few seconds he eased her back and to one side, with his arm still draped around her shoulders, and said to me in a scratchy voice, "What the hell's the matter with you? I told you to take her to the Doyles'."

"You told me some other things, too," I said. "That you were going to notify the state and federal agencies about the kidnapping, for one."

"Listen . . ."

"No, you listen. Marian and I have a pretty good idea what's going on in that head of yours and we're going to sit down and talk about it, the three of us, while there's still time."

"What do you think you know?"

"Pat, for Christ's sake, sacrificing yourself won't bring Chuck back. And even if it could, you can't make that decision alone. You can't go through with it alone."

"He's right, darling," Marian said. "It's my choice, too. I won't let you shut me out."

He glared at me a little longer, but the glare lacked heat now. He stroked Marian's hair, then turned away from her and went back into the living room.

She followed him and I followed her. Big, stucco-walled room furnished in a Spanish motif — wall hangings, tiles, pottery jars. Heavy drapes were drawn across the front window. Dixon sank onto a massive leather couch; Marian sat beside him and took his hand. I moved over to stand facing them in front of a tile-trimmed fireplace.

Nobody said anything. Up to me, I thought. Get him to admit it, that's the first step.

"What time did Latimer call you, Pat?"

His head jerked up. But he lost the rigid

posture almost immediately; his shoulders slumped and he used his free hand to maul his head in that way he had. His jaw, though, retained its stubborn jut.

"What time, Pat?"

"Tell him," Marian said, "for heaven's sake!"

"Few minutes before nine," he said, as if the words were being ripped out of his throat. "Not long before you called from Judson's."

"Did he give you any idea where he was?"

"No. In transit, he said."

"He let you talk to Chuck?"

"Briefly."

Marian's fingers dug at him. "He was all right?"

"Scared, that's all."

"What'd Latimer say to you?" I asked.

"He said if I wanted to see my son alive again, I'd do exactly what he told me. Exactly. He stressed the word more than once."

"Go on. What else?"

"Don't tell anyone that he had Chuck — no one, even Marian. Don't talk to anyone in my office, or to the police or the FBI. Don't leave the house until I heard from him again, some time after five o'clock. He wouldn't call again before that."

"Has he called since five?"

"Not yet."

"What happens when he does?"

"He'll tell me where to meet him. Someplace not too far away, I think."

"What makes you think so?"

"Something he said. That it wouldn't be long after I heard from him again that I'd be seeing Chuck."

"And trading places with him."

"No. That's not what Latimer wants."

"Isn't it?"

"Money. Ten thousand dollars —"

"Bullshit, Pat. He wants you."

Dead air. I imagined I could hear it crackle.

"You," I said again. "You turn yourself over to him and he'll release the boy unharmed — that's his bargain, right? Your life in exchange for Chuck's."

A little more dead air. Then with bitterness, anger, resignation, "It's the only way."

"He's a madman. You really believe he'll release Chuck unharmed?"

"Why wouldn't he? It's me he's after, you said it yourself."

"That's right. He wants you dead. But he also wants you to suffer, maybe more than you're suffering right now. What better way to accomplish that than to kill your son, too?"

Marian made a pained sound. Dixon glared at me with heat again. "That's a god-damn brutal way to put it."

"I meant it to be brutal. Don't tell me the prospect hasn't occurred to you."

It had occurred to him, all right. So had another possibility, I was certain, one that had been on my mind — and surely Marian's — from the beginning and that none of us had spoken aloud or would for the duration. That Chuck's life had already been snuffed out and what Latimer intended to present to Dixon was the boy's dead body. I kept clinging to the conviction that Chuck alive was Latimer's insurance policy, his way out in the event Dixon opted to call in the law or if anything unforeseen happened. But he was pathological — that was the bottom line. It was a crapshoot that logic or rational thought would dictate anything he did.

Dixon was still wallowing in denial. He said vehemently, "I won't let anything happen to Chuck."

"No? How're you going to stop it?"

"There are ways. I've had training."

"Take a hideout gun along? You wouldn't have a chance to use it."

"I'll find a way."

"Only if you catch Latimer by surprise,

and you know that's not likely to happen. He'll figure on you being armed and he'll be armed, too. He's crazy but he's not stupid."

"I have to take the gamble, don't you see that? I've been over this and over it. It's the only way Chuck has any hope of survival. If anybody shows up except me, he'll kill the boy right away. One whiff of the law and my son is dead. Latimer's exact words, and I believe him. He's an animal, he doesn't care about a damn thing except revenge, not even his own miserable hide, and if I don't . . . if I let him . . ." Dixon ran out of words. Things moved in his face, dark things; he mauled his hair again. The hunted eyes appealed to me, then to Marian, to please for God's sake understand.

Across the room, the telephone rang.

It was like a siren going off in the emotion-charged confines — overloud, tearing at frayed nerve ends. We all reacted to it, Dixon the most violently. He was off the couch and racing for the phone while the echoes of the first ring were still bouncing off the stucco walls. He swept up the receiver as the second jangle started, almost knocking the base unit off its stand.

"Yes?" he said, and listened, and the adrenaline rush left him all at once, putting his body into a sag. He leaned a shoulder

271

against the wall before he said, "Why do you — ? What? He told you to call here? . . . All right, yes. Yes."

He took the receiver from his ear, held it away from him as if it were something he was in a hurry to be rid of. "Your assistant," he said, talking to me. "Urgent, she says."

I was at his side by then. He said "Make it quick" as I took the receiver, but the words were nothing I needed to have told to me so I didn't acknowledge them.

"Got your connection," Tamara said. "K. M. Dusay. Latimer's wife's maiden name be Kathryn Marie Dusay."

"Good work. Anything more from Felicia?"

"No."

"You mind standing by a while longer?"

"Long as you need me."

I rang off, returned to where Dixon and Marian were supporting each other near the fireplace. "You can't carry the burden alone," she was saying to him. "Shutting me out like that . . . what were you thinking?" He shook his head and she said, "I couldn't stand to lose both of you."

"You won't lose either of us."

"She will if you don't listen to reason," I said.

"Reason. What reason?"

"What Marian just said. What I've been saying."

"Talk, talk, it doesn't change anything." He disengaged himself, stalked to where a loaded bar cart was pushed up against one of the walls. "Christ, I need a drink."

"No, you don't. You need to keep a clear head."

"Yeah. Don't you think I know that?"

"Here's something you don't know. I've got an idea where Latimer's holding Chuck."

He came around fast and jerky, movements that were almost feral. "What did you say?"

"You heard me."

"Where? Jesus . . . where?"

"Half Moon Bay. Latimer's been living out there. That's what the call from my assistant was about."

"How did you — ?"

"Never mind. Not important now."

He came over to me. "You have an address?"

"Yes, but I'm not going to give it to you yet."

That brought him right up in my face. His breath and his sweat were both sour — the smells of desperation and fear. "You have no right to keep that from me. No right, you hear? Where in Half Moon Bay?"

"Calm down —"

"Screw that. *Where?*"

He started to put his hands on me; I pushed him off. "Listen to me. I won't tell you because I don't want you doing something crazy, like rushing out there. I don't *know* it's where Latimer is or Chuck is. Call it a strong hunch based on —"

"Hunch? Christ!"

"That's right, but given what we know about Latimer, it has a solid basis. He must've risked driving all the way back to the Bay Area or he wouldn't have said what he did to you. Why run that risk instead of holing up somewhere in the mountains or the foothills, making you drive a hundred, two hundred miles to get to him? Much safer for him if he'd done it that way."

Dixon had nothing to say. But he was listening, struggling with the ragged edges of his control.

"Whatever his plan is," I said, "chances are he wants to work it on familiar territory. Chances are, too, the place he rented in Half Moon Bay has some degree of privacy. He'd feel safe there. As far as he knows, nobody is on to the fact that he was living on the coast, much less has the address. He used a different name when he rented it."

I was getting through to Dixon, finally; I could see it in his eyes. Marian helped by taking his arm and saying, "It makes sense, Pat. Can't you see this may be our best hope of getting Chuck back safely?" He looked at her, sucked in a raspy breath, and then did that hair thing again, using his knuckles this time. Thumping his head with them as if he realized how close to coming apart he'd been and was trying to knock some sense back into himself.

"All right," he said. "All right."

"You're not in this alone," I said, "and you can't tackle Latimer alone. Has that gotten through to you?"

Jerky head bob. "But what can you or anybody else do? If Latimer is in Half Moon Bay, if that's where he wants me to come, you can't go along. I told you what he said —"

"There's another way."

"What way?"

"I go out there ahead of you. Leave right away."

It didn't compute. His head wagged this time.

"To check out the address," I said. "If Latimer's there, I should be able to tell it."

"Then what? You're not thinking of —"

"Going in after him myself? No, of course not. Set up a surveillance. Look for a way to

275

get at him, some sort of weak spot we can exploit."

"Suppose there isn't one?"

"We'll still have one thing working for us. The element of surprise. Two of us coming at him, when he expects only you."

"How do we use the advantage?"

"We'll figure that out later. Depends on what I find when I get out there. Circumstances."

"If he sees you, becomes even a little suspicious —"

"He won't. I've got better than thirty years' experience at this kind of thing."

Dixon indulged in more scalp-rubbing. "And while you're checking the address, what do I do?"

"Just what you've been doing. Wait for his call."

"It might be hours. I can't stand much more waiting, not knowing. Look at me. . . . I'm half crazy already."

"You'll know what I know as soon as I find it out. Where I am, what I'm doing."

"You mean we confer by phone."

"Right. I've got a mobile unit in my car, and if you have a second line here —"

"We do. Fax line in my office."

"I'll call you on that line when I get there and we'll keep it open. You let me know as soon as you hear from Latimer. Cell phone in your car?"

"Yes."

"Good. When you leave here we'll stay in touch on that line, no matter where he tells you to go."

"Suppose it's not to Half Moon Bay?"

"No profit in worrying about that now. One step at a time."

Abruptly he moved away, took a couple of restless turns around the room. Thinking it over, weighing it. Pretty soon he stopped and asked Marian, "What do you think?" which surprised me a little. If she had the same reaction she didn't show it.

"It's better than the other way," she said. "It's *something.*"

"All right," he said to me, "we'll do it your way. But I'll tell you one thing right now — I'm not going to Half Moon Bay or anywhere else without a gun."

Marian said, "Pat . . ."

"No. There's no argument on that issue."

"Your choice," I said. "As long as you use restraint."

"I'm no cowboy with a handgun, don't worry about that. What about you? You carrying?"

"I will be. Colt .38 in my car. And I'm not a cowboy, either."

"Okay," he said. "Okay."

We exchanged phone numbers. Two minutes after that, I was back in the car and rolling.

18

The fastest route to Half Moon Bay from the Dixon house was south out of the city on Highway 280, then across Crystal Springs Reservoir and up through the coast range on 92. The drive took about forty-five minutes, and when it was done I was gritty-eyed and hungry again and badly in need of some kind of stimulant. Long, hard, bad day. And the way things were shaping up, the night could turn out to be worse. Much worse.

Latimer worried me the most, but Pat Dixon was a close second. He'd seemed better when I left, in full control again. But the strain had taken its toll, and the longer he had to wait for Latimer's call, the more strung out he was likely to become. Stress affects different people in different ways, and in some it makes them unpredictable in their actions and reactions. Dixon struck me that way. I did not like the idea of him bringing a weapon, but if I'd protested, it would have only made him more determined and he'd have snuck it along anyway. In any event, it wasn't my place to dictate to him. The thing for me to do was to keep him as calm as possible, thinking clearly — when we talked on the phone and when we were together again. If we got into a confrontational situation where the guns came out, I'd take over if necessary and let the weight of the consequences fall on my shoulders.

A hell of a burden to even think about. But I'd dealt myself into this and I had better be prepared; the name of the game was survival.

On the edge of town I made a quick stop at a convenience store, to buy a couple of nutrition bars and a large container of coffee. I needed the coffee in order to stay alert. In the car again I shuffled through my collection of maps, found the one for San Mateo County, and looked up Bluffside Drive. It was off Highway 1 a couple of miles south of the town proper, a squiggly line that meandered through what looked to be open country, ran along close to the ocean for a short ways, and then dead-ended. Not much more than a mile in total length. Could be a lot of houses out there, could be only one or two.

Sipping coffee, I drove on through town to the coast highway and turned south. It was overcast here, as it often is along this coastal stretch no matter what the time of year. No fog tonight, though, just a lot of high gray clouds that gave the Pacific a sullen, monochromatic aspect and a stiff wind that roughened and whitecapped it. Bad luck there. Fog, particularly the kind of thick mist that obscures shapes and deadens sounds, would have given us another advantage.

After a mile and a half by the odometer I slowed to make sure I didn't miss the highway sign for Bluffside Drive. No problem on that score; I spotted the sign in plenty of time to ease into the turn. Three houses were clustered on the south side near the intersection. I peered at the roadside mailboxes as I slid past. On one of the boxes was the number 75 in reflector yellow, which meant that 850 was some distance farther along, close or closer to the ocean.

There weren't any more houses in the immediate vicinity. Cypress trees and then a field of artichokes on the south. On the north, several acres of pumpkin vines stretching seaward. Pumpkins are a major crop in the Half Moon Bay region. The town holds a pumpkin festival every fall to celebrate the harvest; Kerry and I had come down for it once, watched the judging for the largest of the season. First-prize winner had been a 960-pound monster —

Mind wandering. Stay focused!

I passed another house, then a fairly good-sized farm. The farm address was 400. Ahead the road hooked left and appeared to run along a line of low bluffs; I could hear the pound of the surf when I reached that point, even with the windows shut. Once I negotiated the curve, in the crook of which was a windbreak of bark-peeling eucalyptus where a long-gone ranch or farm had been, I had a clear look along the last quarter of the road. Three . . . no, four houses, set well apart from one another on the ocean side.

Immediately I pulled off onto the verge, into the shadow of the eucalyptus grove. The houses were all small, built of salt-grayed wood or cinder block and showing signs of minimal upkeep; the nearest had a yardful of rusting junk cars. Not much vegetation around or between any of them, their back sides openly exposed to the mercy of the Pacific and its sometimes violent winter storms. From what I could see from this vantage point, the low bluff walls were sheer; even if there was a beach down below, and paths leading up from it, you'd be in full view once you got to the top. The logistics weren't any better on the inland side. Mostly open fields; some trees, some cover, but not enough to hide a car for a lengthy surveillance or to shield a man crossing from there to the houses.

Once I'd taken all that in I put the car into a U-turn, not too fast, and drove back around the curve to where I'd seen a track leading in among the trees. A farm road once, overgrown now and blocked after about thirty yards by the remains of a wind-toppled tree, but it would serve my purpose well enough. I made sure Bluffside Drive was empty and then reversed onto the track and in far enough to clear the road and shut off sight of the pumpkin farm to the east.

The first thing I did then was to unclip the .38 and slip it into my jacket pocket. For the next couple of minutes I sat finishing the coffee and sifting through options. One way or another, I had to find out which of the houses was 850 and whether or not it was occupied. The easy way was to drive down there past them, check the mailboxes, turn around where the road dead-ended, and drive back — a traveler who'd lost his way. That would work well enough in most circumstances, but not this one. Latimer knew me and my car; if he was watching, or if the sound of the car passing caused him to look out, he might recognize it. I could not take that chance with Chuck's life in the balance.

Wait until dark? It would be less of a risk then, but still not one I was willing to take. Besides, full dark was at least an hour away. I couldn't just sit here that long, waiting and not knowing if I was right to even be here.

One other option, as far as I could figure, that might work all right if light and angle and distance were what they needed to be. But it would take some time and I owed the Dixons a call first, to let them know the situation.

I tapped out Pat's fax-line number; he answered instantly. "Christ, we've been frantic," he said. "Is Latimer there?"

"I don't know yet." I explained it to him, and he groaned and cursed when I was done.

"What're you going to do? You can't just drive by. . . ."

"I don't intend to." I told him what I had in mind. "We'll keep this line open. I'll get back to you as soon as I can."

"Hurry, will you?"

I laid the handset on the seat, got out and locked the door and then opened the trunk and took out the cased Zeiss binoculars I keep in there. Finding a route through the trees to the south took about three minutes. When I got to where I had an unobstructed view of the houses I adjusted the focus on the glasses and scanned the mailboxes first, one after the other. The binoculars were powerful, 7 x 50; I saw the boxes clearly, but the only one where the angle was right — the nearest — had no number on its visible side. I moved right as far as I dared, then back the other way from the road, but that didn't work, either. I still couldn't make out a number.

I studied the houses themselves. The one I wanted was not the closest; in addition to the junk cars, its yard was strewn with kids' tricycles and wagons. The second in line showed pale light behind curtains drawn over both front windows. The door to its detached garage was closed and there was no vehicle in sight. Number three appeared dark and uninhabited, with shutters up over its facing windows; no car there, either. Number four also showed light — one window uncovered, the other with drawn blinds — and the butt end of a vehicle was just visible at the far corner of the porch. The distance was too great and the angle just a little too oblique for me to be able to read the license number, but the car seemed to be a station wagon and the color was definitely blue.

Number two or number four if he's here, I thought. If I could just get a better angle on the mailboxes . . .

Beyond the eucalyptus was an open, rocky field, and off to the east about forty yards the ground rose into a projection some twenty feet high and sheer-sided where it fronted the ocean, like the prow of a ship. I went in that direction, working my way to the eastern edge of the grove, paralleling and passing beyond the projection. Only the roof of the fourth house was visible from that point. Fine — if the fourth house was Latimer's.

Decision time. In order to get to where I could crawl up the sloping back of the projection I would have to cross better than twenty yards of open ground. And that would put me in full view, if at a long and oblique angle, of anybody looking out from inside the second house. Twice, going and coming back. But there was no other way to do it that wouldn't involve a prohibitive amount of cross-country maneuvering on private property.

Risk it? I took another look at number two's windows; the curtains on both seemed tight-pulled, no edges peeled back, and there was nobody outside. Have to do it, I thought. Everything Dixon or I did tonight involved risk, and this was as minimal as any was likely to be.

I cased the binoculars, wrapped the straps around the case, held it in tight against my left side as I left the cover of the trees. Out in the open, the sea wind was icy and buffeting; its salt-and-kelp smell burned in my nostrils. Walk, steady plodding pace — you're somebody local, somebody who belongs. Don't look at the houses. Straight to the back side of the projection . . . okay.

I was breathing hard, as if I'd just run a long distance. I took several deep, slow breaths before I got down on all fours and crawled up over stubbly grass and sharp juts of rock to just below the rim. Then I uncased the glasses again and eased up the rest of the way on my belly, keeping my head as low to the ground as I could, until I had vision of the houses.

Maybe I could be seen lying up there and maybe I couldn't; it was hard to gauge. Daylight was fading and the light quality was growing poor. Point in my favor, point against me. Get it done fast. I leaned up slightly on my forearms, fitted the glasses to my eyes, got them focused, located a mailbox. On its front was a black-painted number; I could just make it out.

850

The second house, one of the lighted ones, was Latimer's.

He was here. And if Chuck was still alive, he was here, too.

I slithered back below the rim, repacked the binoculars. There was sweat all over me, but the chill wind had dried most of it by the time I was on my feet and moving back — slow and steady — to the trees, hiding the case against my right side this time. When I reached the grove I quickened my pace as much as I dared; thickening shadows made the footing uncertain in there.

Inside the car, I picked up the phone receiver and said Dixon's name.

"No, it's Marian." Her voice was thin, stringy from the pressure. "Pat's gone."

"Latimer called?"

"A minute or two after Pat talked to you."

"How long ago was that? I'm not tracking time too well."

"About twenty minutes. You were right — he's on his way to the coast."

"Half Moon Bay?"

"Princeton. A service station."

"You're sure Latimer sent him to Princeton?"

"That's what Pat said."

"To wait at this service station for another call?"

"Yes. Where are you?"

"Not too far from there."

"Latimer? Is he — ?"

"I'm pretty sure he's here."

Pause. Then, "What are you and Pat going to do?"

"Not sure yet. We'll work something out."

"Be careful. Please."

"You know we will. Stay by the phone."

"What else can I do."

"If you're religious, you might pray a little."

"I've done nothing but since Pat left."

I broke the connection, punched out Dixon's cell phone number. He answered by saying, "Man, what took you so long?"

"I had to do some maneuvering to get an angle on the houses."

"Did you pinpoint Latimer's? Is he there?"

"Looks like it. It's one of the lighted ones."

"Thank God. Marian tell you he's sending me to a Chevron station in Princeton?"

"She told me. Keep you dangling a while longer — and he doesn't want you knowing his address too far in advance."

"That's what I figured, too. Sly son of a bitch."

"How much time did he give you to get to Princeton?"

"An hour. He'll call the station at nine exactly."

"Tight schedule, but you should make it all right."

"Tell me where you are," he said.

"Road a couple of miles south of Half Moon Bay. No more than fifteen minutes from Princeton."

"Suppose I come straight there instead? I can get to you before nine —"

"No. If you're not at the station when he calls —"

"He'll just think I got hung up in traffic."

"More likely it'd make him suspicious. Do what he told you to — straight to the Chevron station, take his call."

No response.

"Pat? You know I'm right."

". . . Yeah. Okay. You going to tell me the name of the road now?"

"Let Latimer do that. Follow his lead all the way."

I thought Dixon might argue, but he didn't. He said, "When I do get there, how're we going to work it?"

"Couple of ideas, but they need more thought." I didn't add that neither had much appeal. Damn tricky to pull off, either of them, and no way I could see yet to minimize the danger.

"I've got a couple myself," he said. "Thresh 'em out now?"

"No, it's too soon. You work on yours, I'll work on mine. Call me as soon as you hear from Latimer and we'll start setting something up then."

"Right."

I sat fidgeting, trying to refine one or the other plan to the point where it seemed viable enough to put into operation. Outside, the shadows got longer, the overcast sky duskier. Past the fenced pumpkin field across the road, I could see part of the ocean and part of the horizon and daylight still showed out there. But it would be gone in another twenty minutes or so, full dark in not much more than half an hour. Full dark by the time Dixon arrived.

Advantage in that, and in favor of the best — by a hair — of my two ideas, which was for me to get into the trunk of Pat's car with my gun out and ready and the trunk lid closed but not latched. Chances were Latimer wouldn't think to search the car, but if he did, I could nail him then and there. If he let Dixon walk straight into the house, I'd wait a couple of minutes, then slip out and find a way to get inside myself and take Latimer by surprise. It might work, but there were any number of things that could go wrong with it, too many ifs and too many variables. The main variable was Latimer himself.

What did he have in mind for Dixon? Another boobytrap bomb? Not if he continued to wait in the house for Pat to arrive; he wouldn't risk blowing himself up. Bombs were not only his MO but a central part of his psychological makeup — yet as much as he seemed to hate Dixon, and as frustrated as he had to be after what had happened at Deep Mountain Lake, he might be looking for a face-to-face finish with a gun or some other weapon. And what about Chuck? If the boy was even still alive . . .

The more I worked my brain, the more uneasy I grew. It was as if my thoughts were on a loop: they kept coming back to Latimer and his mania for explosive devices. But that was not the only thing bothering me about this setup.

Why Princeton?

Princeton was a seaside hamlet five miles or so north of Half Moon Bay. Why send Dixon there instead of to Half Moon Bay proper, a service station closer to Bluffside Drive? That would accomplish the same purpose, wouldn't it?

Or would it?

Fifteen minutes, instead of five or ten.

Was there any reason for him to need an extra five or ten minutes?

Suppose . . .

Christ!

I jerked my watch up close to my eyes; the luminous hands read 8:48. I got the phone to my ear, thumbed the redial button.

"Pat, where are you now?"

"Highway One, couple of miles below Princeton. Why? Did something happen — ?"

"No. Listen, when Latimer calls the station, don't bother to let me know. Just come ahead."

"But I thought we were going to —"

"We'll talk when you get here."

I disconnected before he could say anything else and quit the car, taking the binoculars with me and leaving the door unlocked this time. It was night under the tall trees; I had to pick my way along the route I'd used before, to keep from stumbling over hidden obstacles. When I came to the edge of the grove I checked my watch again. 8:56. Not much light left anywhere now and what there was lay in a pale strip along the western horizon. Inshore the sky was a restless gray-black and the row of houses, even the two lighted ones, were indistinct silhouettes. I withdrew the glasses, focused them on Latimer's cinder block. Zeiss makes the best binoculars in the world; as poor as the dying light was, the magnification was still so fine I could see the front door, the curtained windows with their fringe spill of lamp glow, more or less clearly.

I lowered the binoculars for another quick check of my watch — just nine o'clock — and then leaned a steadying shoulder against a eucalyptus bole and watched the houses through the glasses. One minute, counting the seconds off inside my head. Two minutes. Two and a half —

The porch light came on.

The door opened and Latimer walked out.

No mistake; his head was up and the outside light slanted across his face. Latimer. Alone, and carrying a small suitcase in one hand.

He didn't pause to lock the door. He came straight down the steps, veered to his right to the detached garage and hauled up the door. The rented Toyota was inside; I could just make out the bulky shape of its rear end. Latimer vanished into the shadows on the driver's side.

I waited long enough to see exhaust vapor billow out when he started the engine. Then I was off and running back through the trees.

19

For a little time it was like rushing through a nightmare wood, blind and stumbling. If the eucalypti hadn't been widely spaced I might have done myself some damage; as it was, I managed by luck and intuitive radar to get to where I could make out the shapes of the fallen tree and the car beyond it with only a couple of trip-and-staggers and no falls. Haste was imperative, the only thing on my mind.

My feet got tangled in some strips of peeled bark as I climbed over the downed tree; I kicked loose, doglike, and lurched to the car. I slid under the wheel, tossing the binoculars onto the backseat. The keys dangled from the ignition where I'd left them. I got the engine going and the car moving within a few seconds, making a conscious effort not to jazz the throttle and surge ahead too fast. The machine rocked and bounced in the ruts and then I was out onto the road, angled straight across, blocking it about twenty yards from the curve. There was still room to get around on both sides, but not without easing off slow onto rough ground.

I jammed on the parking brake, shut off the motor and pulled the key out and flipped the trunk release. When I was free of the car, I could hear him coming, a low rumble just distinguishable above the cry of the wind and the beat of the surf. Close but not too close yet; driving fast enough from the sound of it. I ran back and leaned into the trunk and pawed in the carton in the back corner and dragged out one of the pairs of emergency handcuffs I keep in there. Stuffed them into my pocket, banged the lid down.

The Toyota's headlights were visible on the blacktop now, laying down a whitish sheen that extended to the fence posts and lengths of wire separating the road's edge from the pumpkin field.

I ran away from the car, back toward the trees so the Toyota's lights wouldn't pick me out when Latimer made the turn. Something on the .38 snagged in my pocket as I tried to free the weapon; I cursed and yanked hard, heard the faint ripping of cloth as it tore loose. Then it was out and tight in my fingers and I was in a half crouch in the grass and shadows a few yards off the road, a dozen yards from my car.

The engine whine grew louder; the headlamp beams began their sweep as he drove into the curve. The instant I saw the Toyota's nose I knew he wouldn't be able to stop in time straight on. I was up and already starting forward when the lights threw the shape of my car into bright relief.

Latimer stood on the brakes, cramping the wheel to the left to protect his side from impact — the instinctive reaction I'd counted on. Tires and stressed brake linings screeched; the station wagon slid sideways into my car in a three-quarters broadside. Not hard enough to raise much noise or do much damage to either one, but with sufficient force to stall the Toyota's engine, knock something off one or the other's body. There was a metallic clatter on the pavement as I ran up on Latimer's side with the gun extended. The driver's door wasn't locked. I yanked it open with my left hand, my mouth coming open at the same time to yell at him to freeze where he sat.

He should've been confused, if not stunned or hurt; I should've been able to get him under the gun and keep him there. But it didn't work that way. He was already moving when I opened the door, lunging straight up at me, his face twisted and shining masklike in the dome light. I did not have enough time to set myself or to pull the

.38 back out of the way; he plowed into me and one hand struck my arm above the wrist, dislodged the piece and sent it flying. He wedged his shoulder into my sternum, wrapped his arms around my body, and drove me backward and then down under his weight.

If he'd been bigger, if I had landed on the blacktop, it might have been over then and there — for me. The back of my head banged into the ground, but it was mostly thick grass there on the verge, and that cushioned the impact. Still, my vision went out of whack; light and dark images danced and collided and swam apart. He was still on top of me, spitting and snarling in my face, one of his hands groping for my crotch. I bucked him off. But he was back before I could roll over and lever myself up into some kind of fighting position. Pinning me down with torso and legs, swinging with both hands.

Even flat on my back I was able to fend off most of the blows. You can't get much leverage or power behind a punch at close quarters. But I still couldn't see very well; he was just a dark blur in front of my face. I blocked two more swings, but the one after that got through and slammed into my Adam's apple. Pain erupted; I thought in that first instant that he'd crushed something in there. I couldn't breathe, couldn't swallow, couldn't move my head.

His big mistake was in not following up, because in those first few seconds after the blow landed I was pretty much helpless. Only he didn't know that, didn't realize where or how hard he'd hit me, and in the darkness and sweaty heat of battle he couldn't see me pawing at my throat. All he knew was that I was flopping around, kicking my legs, and that I was bigger and stronger than him, even if he did have fifteen years on me; he wanted no more of this kind of give-and-take. The punches stopped coming. He was off me then, and through the blood-pound in my ears I could hear him scrambling away, then beating frantically at something nearby.

The fence. Trying to get over the fence.

I rolled over, shoved onto my knees. My vision was no longer cockeyed, but ghosts kept fluttering at the edges and I was trying to look through them and through a haze of sweat; it took a few seconds to get a bead on Latimer. He was over the fence by then, stumbling off among the pumpkin vines. Ex-military man, ex-con, vicious murderer — fleeing across a pumpkin field like a frightened rabbit.

It took two tries to get on my feet. I could breathe all right through my nose, but my throat was on fire; pain pulsed up into my skull with the first step I took, kept on pulsing in harsher surges as I staggered to the fence. I could not climb the thing — my body wouldn't respond that way. Latimer had bent the fence inward making his climb, so I went through it at the same point, bending wire and uprooting posts, knocking it flat the way a tractor or a tank would. Ahead, Latimer was looking back and he saw me coming; it must have been a hell of a fearful sight because he tripped in his haste and fell and then scuttled like a crab before he was able to regain his feet.

The field was mostly plowed earth and vines and developing fruit. The going wasn't too bad as long as you stayed in between the rows. I had a head of steam up, and when Latimer stopped and then bent and groped along the ground for something to use as a weapon, I knew I had him. Panic had taken him over, and panic loses a two-man confrontation — most other confrontations — nearly every time.

He came up with a rock or dirt clod, flung it at me as I barreled in on him. It missed wide, but I would not have slowed unless it had struck me square in the face; I didn't even turn my head aside. That was the last straw for Latimer. He broke and ran again, this time in a veer toward the bluffs, as if his terror was driving him to seek escape by a plunge into the sea.

I caught him before he'd gone another twenty yards.

The rest of it was anticlimactic. He threw obscenities along with a few punches, but fighting with your hands and your mouth at the same time is a loser's game. I hit him twice in the face and once over the heart, and the heart shot put him down on all fours. He crawled around in a confused way, like a wounded animal, until I put a foot in the middle of his back and flattened him. Then he quit moving and just lay there, sucking air in gasps louder than mine, while I straddled him and hauled out the handcuffs and snapped them over his wrists.

The next few seconds were lost time, a blackout period induced by intense stress and its sudden release. When I came out of it, I was on my feet and dragging Latimer back toward the fence, one hand bunched in the material of his jacket. We were almost there before I grew aware of the headlights fast approaching on Bluffside Drive.

Dixon, I thought. Better be. I'm in no

shape to deal with strangers.

It was Dixon. Whatever he was driving bucked to a halt with the headlights shining close on my car and the Toyota. Not that he had any other choice; the way the impact had left the two machines jammed together, there was no room to drive around on either side. He came out in a hurry. He must've seen me — I was at the fence by then, the section of it that I'd knocked down — but he went straight to the station wagon, leaned his body inside. Looking for his son. I'd have done the same thing if the boy were mine.

Once he'd convinced himself Chuck wasn't there, he backed out and headed my way. I was half dragging, half lifting Latimer's limp form over the wire when he reached us. He looked at me, looked at Latimer, and said in anguished tones, "What happened, what's Latimer doing here? Where's Chuck?"

I tried to tell him, but my voice box wouldn't work; all that came out of the burning in my throat was a barely audible croak. I touched my Adam's apple to let him know I was hurt and he nodded jerkily. Then I gestured at Latimer, semiconscious and groaning; gestured at the cars, saying mutely that Dixon should help me haul the prisoner over there.

He understood, all right, but the only thing on his mind was his son. He wagged his head, backed off a step. "The house . . . how far is the house?"

I got words out this time in a broken whisper. "Pat, listen to me . . ."

He wouldn't have listened if I'd shouted at the top of my voice. He said, "I have to know if he's all right," and turned on his heel and ran for the road.

Shit!

I let go of Latimer, hopped free of the fence, and went after Dixon.

On the blacktop his stride faltered briefly as his head swiveled toward his car and the other two blocking it. Then, like a long-distance runner shifting gears, his body bent forward and he was into an all-out sprint. He was in good condition, and he had long legs and the impetus of a father's fear for his child; he began to pull away from me immediately. Even before he reached the straight stretch beyond the curve, he was eating up ground and widening the gap between us at an alarming rate.

At first I ran with one hand massaging my throat, in an effort to work off the paralysis so I could yell the right words to make him stop. But even if I'd been able to start my larynx functioning, I didn't have the wind for forceful shouting; the suck-and-blow of my breathing was like noise in a wind tunnel. It took all I had left, as badly used and hurting as I was, to keep up the pursuit. Dixon had left me no choice. I *had* to get to him before he got to Chuck and it didn't matter right then if I collapsed, maybe blew out something vital, in the effort.

More than likely I would have lost the race if he'd known which of the houses was Latimer's. He'd opened up better than a fifty-yard lead by the time he neared the cinder block, but because the fourth house was also lighted and he couldn't be sure which was the right one, he stayed on the road and skidded to a halt at the mailbox in front, just long enough to read the number. I was off the road by then, racing in a long diagonal for the porch. When he came charging along the path and up the porch steps, the distance between us had been chopped nearly in half. Even so, he had the door open and was bulling inside before I reached the strip of weedy front lawn.

Survival instinct shrieked at me to cut it off then and there. Urgency kept me pounding forward. I hit the bottom porch step, used the railing as a fulcrum to propel myself up the rest of the way and into the open doorway. Lights were on all through the interior, but Dixon was nowhere in sight. Then I heard him, in one of the rooms off a short hallway to my left. Involuntarily I ducked my head, hunched my shoulders — and plunged inside, into the hallway.

"Chuck, oh God, Chuckie, it's Dad, I'm here now. . . ."

Second room on the left. I stumbled to the doorway, and Dixon was down on his knees beside a saggy bed with an old metal frame. Chuck lay supine on the bare mattress, spread-eagled with his arms and legs tied tight to the frame, gagged and blindfolded with rags. Dixon reached out to him, crooning.

I got in there, wheezing and shaking from the exertion, and laid both hands on his shoulders and heaved him backward before he could touch the boy. He lost his balance and landed on his buttocks, yelling. "What's the idea? What the hell's the matter with you?"

I put myself between him and the bed, dragging in air with my mouth wide open, rubbing again at my aching throat. The first time I tried to talk, nothing happened. The second time, I was able to make words, cracked but with some force behind them.

They felt bloody coming out, as if they'd torn skin off the walls of my esophagus.

"Bomb in here."

"What!" He stared at me in confused disbelief.

"Chuck . . . the bed . . . wired somehow. Latimer boobytrapped him."

It took a cautious look under and around the bed to convince Dixon. The explosive device was on the floor underneath, packed in a cardboard carton with wires coming out of the far side and snaking, tight with tape, along the bed frame and along Chuck's left arm to the rope that bound his wrist. Cut or pull on those wires and father and son — and me along with them — would've been torn apart by whatever Latimer had put into the carton. Judging from the size of the carton, there was enough black powder and frag in there to blow up the entire house.

"The dirty son of a bitch," Dixon said. He was trembling like a man with palsy. "I ought to go back and kill him for this. I mean it, I ought to blow his miserable fucking head off."

But it was just talk, an expression of the most intense kind of hatred one man can feel for another. He had himself more or less under control and I would not have to go chasing after him again. I left him with Chuck, found the phone in the kitchen and called the SFPD. My voice had come back strongly enough so that I had no difficulty explaining to the night chief of inspectors what we had here. He said he'd get the bomb unit out the fastest way possible, and that he'd take care of notifying the local authorities.

I went to tell this to Dixon, but he was kneeling again beside the bed with his head bowed in an attitude of prayer. He hadn't touched the boy in any way, but he must have talked to him, let him know everything was going to be all right: Chuck lay relaxed now, waiting, secure in the presence of his father. I went away quietly, without saying anything to either of them.

The long walk back up the road left me weak-legged and shambling a little. I'd been running on reserves for some time now and the tank was almost empty. Latimer wasn't where I'd left him, but he hadn't gone far; I spotted him in the pumpkin field again, crawling along crabwise on his belly between two of the rows. He was in much worse shape than I was, still dazed and disoriented, mewling words to himself. I could make out some of what he was mumbling, and it was mostly gibberish dominated by phrases like "make them pay" and "blow him sky high" and "boom boom big boom."

Wrong, Latimer, I thought. This is the way it ends for you.

Not with a boom but a whimper.

20

In the back of the Toyota wagon, among Latimer's jumble of personal effects, the police found half a dozen thick 8½ x 11 spiral-bound notebooks. All were filled with chronological entries in a small, crabbed hand, dating back as far as Latimer's last five months in San Quentin. Pat Dixon had access to the notebooks, and later in the week he let me look through them in the privacy of the D.A.'s office.

They made chilling reading.

Madman's diaries. Psychotic ramblings on every page. The most disturbing thing about them was not the references to me in what he'd written at Deep Mountain Lake and that last evening in Half Moon Bay, but the casual way he spoke of killing as the answer to all his problems — the assumption that he had a moral right to destroy lives, as many lives as he deemed necessary, simply because he felt he'd been wronged.

On the day of his release from prison he'd written, "Free at last. Except that I'm not free, not yet. I won't be free until I make every last one of the bastards pay. Dixon,

Turnbull, Cotter, Kathryn, Strayhorn, their brat, *all of them* for what they did to me. That's all that matters. That's the shining focus of my life from now on. I don't even care if I die in the process as long as I get them first. Vengeance is mine, saith Donald Michael Latimer."

Vengeance is mine. It's an attitude that is becoming more and more prevalent these days — the lunatic's battle cry, the mantra of the alienated, the dysfunctional, the outraged, the fanatical. Me, me, me! they shriek. *I'm* what's important, nothing and nobody else. And all the while they're stockpiling handguns and assault weapons and explosive materials, getting ready to Make Them Pay. And when the pressure becomes too great, the shrieks too deafening in their own ears, out they go to perpetrate as much carnage and mayhem as they can in the name of glorious retribution, in the sick, pathetic certainty that their deaths and the deaths of their victims will have more meaning than their empty lives.

There is something fundamentally skewed about a society that breeds so many psychos of this type; that teaches violence, or at least offers more than a modicum of tacit approval of it, as a viable problem-solving option; that allows some individuals to believe, actually feel morally justified in their belief, that it's all right to slaughter innocent people as a means of Fighting Back or Getting Even.

Reading Latimer's notebooks put all these thoughts in my mind, and led me to express them to Dixon. He agreed. But what can you do about it? he asked me. How do you go about altering the direction of a societal mindset that seems to be edging out of control?

I had no answer for him.

The only answer I had was personal. The one I'd come to accept for myself at Deep Mountain Lake; the one that said, among other things, that vengeance is *not* mine and never would be again. The one that had been around for thousands of years, long before Moses brought it down from the mountain with the nine other commandments.

Thou Shalt Not Kill.

A lot of people saw fit to thank me over the days following Latimer's arrest and Chuck's safe return home, in person and on the phone. Pat, Marian, Chuck, Callie Ostergaard, Mack Judson, even Sheriff Ben Rideout. All the expressions of gratitude embarrassed me; I still felt that if I'd been smarter, or quicker on the uptake, or more cautious, some of what had happened could have been avoided. But the thank-yous were nonetheless good to hear, and not because of any stroking of my ego.

They said to me that maybe society was not so bad off after all, and men like Donald Michael Latimer were only an aberration, not a proliferating mutant breed, and there was still hope for the future, for a genuine kinder, gentler world.

Maybe this was an answer, too. Or part of one.

Caring. Simple caring.

Kerry came home on Saturday afternoon. I picked her up at SFO. She took a long look at me when she got into my abused but still drivable car, one of her analytical studies, but she didn't say anything then about the condition of my face — the bandaged cut over my eye, the bruise on my throat, the various abrasions and contusions. It was not until we'd been at the Diamond Heights condo for a while that she came over and sat on the arm of my chair and did some tender probing of a battered old phiz only she could love.

"Can't even go away on a normal vacation, can you?" she said. More with sadness,

I thought, than exasperation.

"Seems not."

"Why do you always get mixed up in volatile situations like this latest one? Where you end up being hurt in some way?"

"If I knew how to avoid them, I would. I guess I'm a magnet — the negative-attraction kind."

"Maybe, but that doesn't explain why you let yourself become so deeply involved every time. What do you get out of it?"

"Do I have to get something out of it?"

"Well, you must or you wouldn't let it happen."

"What did you get out of roasting your pretty little hinder for eight days in Houston?"

"That's hardly the same thing."

"Bottom line, it is. Answer the question."

"I told you last night. Milo Fisher signed on the dotted line."

"So what you got out of it was a contract for the agency."

"For a major ad campaign."

"Right. A major ad campaign that means a lot more work for you. Eight days out of your life for a piece of paper and the thrill of putting in long hours to benefit a new client, not to mention Jim Carpenter's bank account?"

"Of course not —"

"Money? A bonus or a big raise?"

"Money isn't important to me, you know that."

"Well, then? What did you get out of signing up old Milo Fisher? You personally, not Bates and Carpenter."

"All right, smart guy, you tell me. That's what you're leading up to. What did I get?"

"Satisfaction," I said.

"Oh, is *that* the payoff?"

"Sure it is. That's what you get out of what you do and it's what I get out of what I do. It's why we work so hard, get so involved, care so much. And why we love each other, too. I satisfy you and you satisfy me, sexually and every other way."

"You think so, do you?"

"Don't you?"

We looked at each other. Seeing eye to eye, at last.

Pretty soon she said, "I guess you still hurt a lot."

"Not much now. I guess you're tired after the long trip."

"Not too tired."

"So?" I said.

"So?" she said.

So we went to bed. And some time later Kerry got up and I heard her singing in the shower. I grinned when I recognized the tune and lyrics. Yawned, stretched, and then laughed out loud.

The song was "I Can't Get No Satisfaction."

We hope you have enjoyed this Large Print book. Other Thorndike Press or Chivers Press Large Print books are available at your library or directly from the publishers.

For more information about current and upcoming titles, please call or write, without obligation, to:

Thorndike Press
P.O. Box 159
Thorndike, Maine 04986 USA
Tel. (800) 257-5157

OR

Chivers Press Limited
Windsor Bridge Road
Bath BA2 3AX
England
Tel. (0225) 335336

All our Large Print titles are designed for easy reading, and all our books are made to last.